THE RISE
OF
SAMSON

A BIBLICAL NOVEL

JEFFREY D. MEREDITH

FREILING PUBLISHING

Published by Freiling Publishing, a division of Freiling Agency, LLC.

P.O. Box 1264,
Warrenton, VA 20188

www.FreilingPublishing.com

Paperback ISBN: 978-1-950948-82-6
Library of Congress Number: 9781950948826

Printed in the United States of America

To Megan Alexandra,

A short story about fighting and betrayal hardly seems sufficient for everything you've given me. Even still, it will have to do, and I hope you enjoy it—now at last in print.

Yours,

Jeff

Author's Note

When the Bedouin shepherd Muhammed edh-Dhib discovered the Isaiah Scroll and an assortment of other papyri and parchments in a dry cave near the Dead Sea, he could hardly have known he had in his hands one of the world's great archaeological finds. The ancient writings, preserved undisturbed for thousands of years in sealed clay jars, confirmed the prophetic nature of Scripture's central promise:

> *But he was wounded for our transgressions,*
> *he was bruised for our iniquities:*
> *the chastisement of our peace was upon him;*
> *and with his stripes we are healed.*
> *All we like sheep have gone astray;*
> *we have turned every one to his own way;*
> *and the LORD hath laid on him*
> *the iniquity of us all. (Isaiah 53:5–6, KJV)*

* * * * *

Yet not all the texts were of the inspired sort. Only recently has a small bundle of three obscure Dead Sea Scrolls begun to capture the attention of scholars. Collectively labeled *Testimony of Samson* (for lack of anything better), the manuscripts were found tied together with a nearly disintegrated leather strap in a nondescript jug toward the back of Qumran Cave 7.

"Illiterate Hebrew" according to a skeptical Jewish professor, the collection appears to be a rough translation from Akkadian by a minimally educated scribe, one Berah of Mareshah. It begins with a rather humdrum accounting of the original scrolls' prior owners—a record akin to an old-fashioned library lending card—that in fact reads like a "Who's Who" of ancient great men, starting with King David himself. He apparently seized the scrolls from the Philistines during the sack of Gath, where they would already have been more than fifty years old.

In Judah's library, then, the scrolls remained unmolested for close to four centuries, until that adventurous Egyptian, Pharaoh Necho, triumphed over King Josiah at Megiddo. Taking an assortment of treasure, hostages, and records on his way to Assyria to ensure the Southern Kingdom's good behavior, Necho's leverage was just as quickly lost when a combined Egyptian-Assyrian force was routed at Carchemish by the great Babylonian Emperor Nebuchadnezzar, he who would rule "wheresoever the children of men dwell" (Daniel 2:38).

The Babylonians captured Necho's train, which included *Testimony of Samson* and immeasurable other booty, carrying all back to the royal archives in the treasury at their capital. Presumably, the collection sat neglected for more than 150 years, surviving both the Persian conquest and the first "local" diaspora.

At long last, King Artaxerxes showed mercy to that famous wall builder Nehemiah, releasing his favored cupbearer to the City of David with authority and gifts, including these scrolls. As Nehemiah set about restoring Jerusalem's defenses and reviving God's people, he also assigned translation duties to Berah, though he apparently held the works (or perhaps the man) in little regard. How the three manuscripts came to reside in a jug in a wilderness cave will likely never be discovered.

Now, despite the original scrolls' dubious provenance, Berah appears to have neither marveled at their survivability nor questioned their reliability. *The Rise of Samson* is the first of the three. And though the events written herein seem somewhat fantastic, they hardly break from the spirit of the histories recorded in the Bible's book of Judges, or this particular story's chief belligerent.

Table of Contents

Introduction

Recorded by Berah of Mareshah at the instruction of Nehemiah, a gift of King Artaxerxes from the royal archives of Babylon.

Captured from the caravan of Pharaoh Necho at Carchemish by Nebuchadnezzar, King of Babylon.

Seized from the palace in Judah by Pharaoh Necho upon the death of King Josiah.

Taken from the record keepers at Gath by David, King of Israel.

Recorded at the command of Seranim Occily, Ruler of Gath and all Philistia.

* * * * *

Recorded faithfully by Carmuk, secretary to the council of Philistine lords at Gaza, together with Kordunk the torturer, in obedience to the great Seranim Occily, whose providence once again extends over Ekron, Ashdod, Gath, Ashkelon, Gaza, and the other Philistine territories.

Seranim Occily, et al:

Greetings! In accordance with your wishes, O lord of Gath, the Hebrew dog Samson did consent to provide a thorough accounting of his life, that a complete investigation of his uncommon strength might be concluded. May my lord be patient as I explain the delay in the delivery of this report.

Samson now bears little resemblance to the rabble-rouser who slaughtered the young men of Philistia. Yet in his spirit, no change can be discerned. Though he was promised adjournment from Kordunk's daily chastening in exchange for a submissive testimony—an undeserved mercy in light of his lowly state—even still, his speech is filled with defiance and blasphemy against the honorable Philistine people and the great god Dagon. While much of this abuse was regrettably included in this testimony for the sake of wholeness, such insolence required punishment! Indeed, your own regent, Bogrog, sealed the orders for enhanced beatings with your courtly ring.

Now, let my lord permit further explanation: As per your orders, Samson's confession was invalid unless he gave a blood oath before the altar to Dagon at Gaza. This was assigned to the newly appointed high priest of the city's temple, one Maruck by name, because of his many dealings with the Hebrew—at Timnah, Lehi, and elsewhere—which neither man disputed. However, upon arriving to administer the oath, the priest Maruck did die suddenly, although he appeared in good health beforehand. The other priests viewed this as an unfavorable omen, and were quite unwilling to fulfill the obligation afterwards, in spite of much mockery and provocation from the prisoner.

Furthermore, Samson astounded us when he argued that such and such a vow would be null on account of his service to the Hebrew god—the very god who abandoned him! Therefore, following some discussion between the priests of Dagon and your representatives, Samson was permitted to confirm honorable intent to his own god (and tortured accordingly), though it was agreed upon by all that his words would be held valid.

Seranim Occily, let this explanation satisfy your understandable impatience. Dagon and the whore at Sorek have delivered to us a mighty enemy. By our wits, Samson's confession failed to unearth any new information about the root of his great power. Nevertheless, it is worthy of archiving: Firstly, so the Philistine people might revel in the Israelite's lament; and secondly, to exonerate the scores who fell by his hands.

As a matter of record, I, Carmuk, did question and record this testimony myself in Gaza, and am wholly persuaded it is in earnestness and not disearnestness. While Kordunk is spent from his exertions with the prisoner, he has promised to make sport of Samson at the festival to the great god Dagon in a week's time.

Chapter 1

I hate you. How I hate you.

Lord, how I hate these Philistines and their detestable gods.

Why do you insist on my testimony day after day? That corrupt priest Maruck lorded his position over me, and now he lies cold atop the hearse. Can my words bring him back? Can any explanation restore the pride of the Philistines or the young men I slew with my own hands? Why do you plead with me on my own account, as if you had my interests at heart? Should I care whether my last days are pleasant or miserable?

No, I do not care.

In my present state, one is as good as the other. I am sick of the land. I am sick of the sea. I am sick of the mountains and the valleys. I have had enough of it all. You could bribe me with every virgin in Philistia, if there are any, but the Lord has stricken me; he has quenched my thirst for life, and my time has come. My God, hasten the day.

Even if the Lord had not brought me to ruin, you Philistines have taken my eyes, and I have no mind to beg. But that is not the only reason I hate you.

I know your intentions. I see it as clearly as if I were a young man again—though you have taken my eyes. Your fat Seranim Occily has set his mind to the east, to regain his influence on Israel's choice fields and flocks. I tell you the people there will not welcome him. He ought to fix his gaze farther north, to Assyria, or look south, to Pharaoh and his hordes, lest one of those mighty nations come and seize all he has—right down to his last barrel of beer. I bear witness to the devastation Pharaoh and his legions inflict, like a swarm of locusts, consuming all before them. And without beer, how will your fat king seduce whatever unlucky whore he plucks from his harem for his nightly escapade? Yes, I once had a viewing of your fat lord—in Ashkelon, as will be told in proper course. Truly I have never seen his equal, not among one man or two stacked together! And I know no maiden would willfully lay with such a behemoth, who is as wide as the Rephaites are tall, when her very life would be smothered away in his mounds of flesh.

There is only one thing I desire in these, my final days: *silence*—to be alone with my laments and to remember my father and mother and brothers, my wanderings about the mountains, or the sweet figs and cool streams...

Very well, I will tell you all, though I hate you and curse you, if only for the hope of ensuing silence and of keeping the fingers and toes you have not yet removed. Since you took my eyes and more, and I can no longer journey safely through Israel or set my gaze upon a woman, I despise all. I long for the end of this miserable existence and then to plead my case before my Maker. God willing, I will prod *him* to vengeance.

But as Occily has insisted, I will start my story from the beginning. I will confirm the events you Philistines bore witness to yourselves and reveal the truth behind many rumors—of suffering and betrayal, oppression and murder, wars and desolation, and ruin, ruin all.

Chapter 2

My father and mother were the worthiest of Hebrews. They were tireless in work, paid wages fairly without favoritism, and venerated the Levites properly. Their hearts were charitable to a fault, consenting to bless enemies, including the children of Philistine oil merchants who apportion with false scales and bottom out clay jars with stone. They cry "final sale" or "hottest burning" but dilute their product with donkey semen. Yet neither my mother nor father ever held a grudge, even on the coldest nights when the lamps reeked and fizzled.

My mother's good nature was inborn and refined by a long trial of childlessness and then tested further by much advice on the matter from her mother-in-law. But after she conceded any hope of children, an angel from God appeared to her as she gathered pistachios in the westernmost knoll of our family's grove. There, out of the sight of my father and the other workers, the messenger foretold of a mighty son who would cause grief for the enemies of her people. Tell me: Do you believe the prophecy complete?

My father doubted her story, fearing she had been taken by one of the Rephaim, who were always out and about causing devilry of one sort or another in those days—until their days were cut short. But my mother's virtue was true, and my father's love for her sincere. Thus he questioned her carefully and prayed to God the angel might return.

They said God heard his prayer! My father swore the angel came back that very afternoon, sharing instructions for my upbringing—that I might not cut my hair, drink wine, or eat the unclean food you Philistines revel in. The author of these commands was kept from me for many years, and it was my disobedience of his first order that led to my present suffering.

And if your best men could replicate my deeds by modeling such behavior, and thus win the lasting renown of the Philistine people, they would never consent to do so, for they resist all self-discipline and have no higher virtue than self-indulgence.

Later in life when my fame had grown, my father was overburdened with entreaties from so many sluggards that he was by necessity forced to tighten his fist. However, he never neglected the tithe or worked the outer boundaries of our fields or groves. Nor could any traveling stranger accuse my family of stinginess, though that was to our detriment. My parents forgave debts and offered first fruits at the appointed times, suffered for their charity, were my counselors and comforters in times of trouble...

I could go on, but I choose not to indulge your triumph any further.

That day, my father offered nourishment to the angel, but he would not partake in our sacrifice nor even share his name. Instead, he entered the kindling fire where a goat steak cooked, then rode the flames to heaven. Seeing such glorious ascension, my father despaired of life, but my mother's belief never wavered, and in the end her faith was vindicated.

Chapter 3

My family owns property in the hill country of Zorah. In my youth, we harvested grains in the spring; grapes and breba figs in the summer; and then in the fall, pomegranates, pistachios, almonds, and more figs. Though yields never left us wealthy—and the Philistines' highway robbers often seized any surplus we hoped to sell—neither did we want for food. The rewards of our labor secured our comfort through winter.

I spent many happy years at home, playing, exploring, gathering—just as a boy should. Oh! If only I could have been satisfied with the life of a farmer. Walking field and grove, concerning myself with little more than winter rains...I might still be living in simplicity, sowing and harvesting in season. In those days, there were not so many Philistines as now, and it was easy enough to smell one before he hooked 'round a switchback.

Yet God did not destine me to such a fate. If my childhood possessed a certain carefree habit thanks to the abundant caution of my parents, still I neither ate nor drank in contentedness. For which Hebrew was not keenly aware of the suffering of our brothers at your hands? There were seizures and levies in the name of the Seranim, kidnappings and killings without hope of justice, and worst of all, you unleashed the Rephaim upon us. They raped the women, murdered the men, and brutalized children. They were lawless reprobate sons of the devil, and I curse you to hell for their villainy!

Because of this oppression, during the late winter of my eighteenth year, certain elders of Judah and Ephraim conspired to gather the young men of their tribes, to test and strengthen their mettle for Israel and the Lord. The official rationale was a three-day Levitical camp to honor our patriarchs. The event would be led by an experienced soldier named Johannon, a Judahite who made a name for himself serving the king of Edom in his failed uprising against Pharaoh. Young men of Dan were also invited to the gathering, though more for our central location near the valley of Mahaneh Dan than any particular gifting.

This was my first time anywhere far from home besides Shiloh with my parents, and the adventure of a lifetime—or so I thought.

Rather, it became something more. Mahaneh Dan was the crux of everything that followed in my life, right down to this bitter end—every triumph, every disaster, every resentment and crisis and vendetta. They all stemmed from this one journey to that desolate desert valley. That is where I came face to face with the enemy, where I took my first life, and where the Spirit of the Lord grabbed hold of me and led me down an irrevocable path of struggle…

Yet it all started innocently enough.

I traveled with two other boys from my tribe: Isnach, who was shy, and Torgan, a rascal inclined to contradict whatever instruction he received, whether at home or from the Levites. After an agreeable hike over hill and dale, we were within a stone's throw of our destination at Mahaneh Dan when our road steepened rapidly.

We followed ancient steps carved into stone that twisted round the crag, until—at the crest, where the pass snaked its way between two short, jagged peaks—a large boulder had recently fallen, nearly sealing off our pathway. Travelers had little more than a foot to squeeze between obstruction and the sheer cliffside wall. And as we wedged through, we came quite suddenly to a gulch nearly 20 feet across, with a felled cedar for a bridge over the water a dozen feet below.

My traveling companions and I unstrapped our effects at the edge and sidled to the midpoint of the cedar. There we sat in high spirits, spitting and hurtling stones until Torgan spied a mudbug on a rotting branch against one of the stream's banks. Just as quickly, he produced a line and hook from his bag and attached several stale lentils for bait. This he claimed was the creature's favorite meal (apart from rolled goat scat, which we did not have). In short order, he reeled in a dozen or so of the pinchies.

He had just begun to explain what a fine dish they would make, despite what the Levites say, when a group of ten or twelve Ephraimites stole up behind us. Their approach was hidden by the boulder and our laughter. As the entourage squeezed through the pass one by one and came upon the bridge where we sat, their leading man called out, "Shalom, Danites!" He stood on tiptoe, craning his neck to look past us. When he spied no others, he said, "This boulder has blocked our donkeys from proceeding, and they must travel a long way to meet us on the other side. But we are in a rush to Mahaneh Dan, and you are not. Help carry our bags then, will you?"

The Ephraimites were heavily laden, for they formed a sort of chain gang, handing their bags forward one after another around the boulder to the bridge, where the goods piled up quickly. I loathed their entitled authority, and answered accordingly: "We also go to Mahaneh Dan, and only stopped to eat dinner. If you are in a hurry as you say, tote your own luggage. We will make way. Shove on and leave us be."

But the Ephraimites raised their eyebrows and scoffed, "How can Dan stand alongside Ephraim and Judah?" And they jeered and ridiculed us, until their leader—who we quickly gathered was named Macksam—quieted them all. He approached us passively with hands held out—and kicked my pouch of almonds off the edge into the stream below!

"Those were my nuts!" I cried. "What right had you to drown them?"

Nodding to his companions, three of those rogues scooped up our remaining packs and dangled them over the edge. "No rights, but only a trade to beg," Macksam answered. "We are feint with long and hard travel, and deprived of our donkeys. You are at rest, so give us a breather by carrying our luggage carefully across and down the other side. When you have completed the task, we will return the favor and deliver your bags across the bridge. Then we may all part in friendship."

My fists clenched and Torgan glared, but Macksam felt our defiance. "And if there is any chicanery, you and your bags can all take baths together!" Catching sight of Torgan's mudbugs, he scowled and said disgustedly, "You will need a ceremonial cleansing to settle your stew anyway."

"Well, boys," I cried to my companions, "this one is a Levite in disguise. You can tell by his furrowed brow. We had better hurry and do what he says before he demands any other freewill offerings."

We inched back to their side and moved out of their way, glaring as the lot of them sauntered past to the bridge—sneering, laughing, spitting, farting. Macksam said to them all, "What luck that as we lost three asses to one side of the mountain, we found three more on the other."

I burned at these insults! I longed to teach those Ephraimites a lesson. But there were only three of us, and my companions had not the strength for such an unbalanced fight.

Yet God was with us that day, or at least not with our adversaries.

Much to my astonishment, the arrogant Ephraimites made a fatal error. Even now I cannot believe their stupidity, though I concede they were also young—barely older than we were. They all began to cross the cedar in a line together, rather than divide their numbers to ensure our obedience. And they left our bags with the last three to cross, who—not being anxious to hold extra weight—set them down until it was their turn.

Sensing a chance to gain the upper hand, I nodded slightly to Torgan to take his staff, and warned Isnach to support him. "When I give the signal," I whispered, "sweep away the remnant—and if it comes to blows, hit their shins." Because I had learned already that a man will absorb a hard blow with his upper arms, back, or buttocks before he concedes his shinbone.

Quickly I clambered up to the top of the boulder, threw my staff like a javelin to the far side of the gulch, and then called to the Ephraimites walking in a line on the cedar: "Hey, brothers, catch a load!"

With that, I sprung with all my might, flying from the boulder, over the heads of those just entering the bridge, and came crashing down upon the two who were farthest along. They fell into the water, and I nearly went down with them, just barely managing to hang on to the log. This collision jarred the cedar from root to branch, forcing the rest of the Ephraimites to kneel to keep their balance, or else they might have just kicked me off as I hung there.

But I do not think they understood what was happening. Indeed, my leap caught them all by surprise. And as I climbed back atop the bridge, their eyes looked after their brothers below. In vain they reached down to pull up their companions, whose outstretched hands were *just* out of reach. They cried out at me, demanding an explanation.

Back on my feet, I moved the rest of the way across the bridge, grabbed my staff, and stood menacingly, blocking their exit. I cried out, "Torgan now!" and he and Isnach rushed forward, slamming their staff lengthwise like a push broom into the backs of those three Ephraimites who had yet to begin crossing. They were taken completely unaware, and tumbled down to the drink. Having thus secured our bags, Torgan gave the nearest man on the bridge a fierce whack on the back of his leg. That fellow yelped, and in trying to keep his balance, succeeded only in pulling his two nearest companions off the cedar with him. Seven Ephraimites had fallen, and the remaining men were unarmed and pinned entirely between Torgan and me.

"Well, Ephraim, this contest is up," I said. "Will you jump, or shall we play the part of Joseph's brothers and throw you into the well?"

They expressed disbelief that we would carry out the same discipline they had only moments earlier threatened to inflict upon us, and began pleading for mercy—Macksam most of all. They promised to tote our luggage to Mahaneh Dan, and moreover to furnish us richly with steak and barley if only we would let up.

It was Torgan who tired first of their whining; he sent the man nearest him tumbling down with a crippling whack to the knee. He pressed forward to dispatch the next Ephraimite, who wisely jumped before the blow could be delivered.

"You Ephraimites are a bunch of peckerheads!" Torgan yelled. "I wish Jepthah had taken care of all of you!" He struck the next man fiercely across his head. I have seen a fair number of men boxed senseless, and verily believe that fellow would have drowned if not for his companions below catching him in the water.

I moved forward and motioned to strike the man nearest to my side, and he flinched and teetered, fighting desperately to keep his balance, but in the end over-corrected and fell like all the rest.

I laughed heartily at our fallen adversaries, who appeared like pigs wallowing in muck. Such good cheer angered their last man on the cedar, Macksam. "You don't know who I am, Danite," he growled, cursing me fiercely.

Sadly, I did not have the chance to learn then, though I would in the days ahead, much to my regret.

"Macksam, Macksam," I said, shaking my head. "Say Shibboleth." Then I struck him fiercely across the back, so that he tumbled down head over heels.

He came up covered in mud, bleeding and sputtering in fury. "May God deal with me, be it ever so severely—" he screamed, nearly finishing his oath before his friends wisely quieted him. He raged on: "I'll see you unclean dogs boiled alive. You will all be ground to chaff. I know one of the Nephilim, and you will regret—"

"Go to hell, Ephraim!" Torgan interrupted. "You don't scare us with your big talk of big men."

"We ought to throw your bags down, too," I said, "because you are in a hurry."

Upon that threat, Macksam's friends begged him to stop and apologized repeatedly, admitting they had received what they deserved for their intransigence. And we, too, thought better of it, for these fellows would have been after us quite a bit faster if they had fewer possessions to carry. But I gathered from their supplies a generous portion of almonds to compensate for the pouch Macksam kicked over the side, along with other choice morsels.

As I did, quiet Isnach conceived an unlikely "final insult," one that gives me great satisfaction to this very day. "Macksam, catch," he said, lobbing one of Torgan's mudbugs at him. The man jumped to dodge the creature, but Isnach pulled out another and invited his target to prepare himself like a man.

"Don't you dare, you fool!" Macksam cried as Isnach let fly. This shot would have done the best slingers proud: it struck the man square in the head and grabbed hold of his sidelock. He yelped and tried to swat it off, lost his balance, and fell back under water with the mudbug still holding on.

"Who needs a ceremonial cleansing now, you ass!" Torgan taunted, and we all laughed again.

So it was that we regained our bags, conquered the Ephraimites, and hurried on toward Mahaneh Dan, laughing, whooping, and exulting in the joy of victory. Yet it never occurred to us that by dumping those rascals off the bridge, we had saved their lives.

Chapter 4

That evening, we arrived at Mahaneh Dan, a narrow, descending valley well suited to our secret congregation. We made for the Danite standard, exchanging smug looks as we passed the Ephraimites, never imagining their brothers who swam with mudbugs were better off than we. How could we have foreseen the disaster upon us? We were soaring like eagles!

The aroma of goat steaks and lamb spits filled the early evening air; there was singing, wrestling, races, and merry-making. As far as I was concerned, the young men assembled were the pride of Israel. Though our sticks and slings would have been despised by all but the lowliest shepherd, I had never seen such an event. Here, hidden in the desert's desolation, was the makings of an army that would not only throw off the Philistines, but strike fear in Pharaoh's proud heart—or so I believed.

In truth, our assembly was nothing like the days of old, when Joshua led Jeshurun into the Promised Land. Our numbers more closely resembled Gideon's 300, and as I ponder him who threshed wheat in a winepress, I feel his despair.

Before the meat had come off the fire—before we'd sung Jehovah's praise or honored our patriarchs—a large contingent of armed Philistines arrived. The Lord curse the Hebrew who sold out his brothers for their silver. These fellows were not the usual brigands, either, but soldiers with iron armor and weapons. Some were mounted on Egyptian warhorses; these carried long iron-tipped spears. Worst of all, they were accompanied by three Rephaites. This was the first time I saw one of those big fellows up close, and though I was over six feet tall, I suddenly understood what it meant to feel like a grasshopper. They towered over us like trees, and their dark eyes burned with unquenchable anger and violence and lust. Even without heavy spears, they might have trampled us all.

The whole contingent barged into the center of our camp, where the Philistine commander demanded angrily, "What is this unregistered gathering?" as he kicked over a boiling meat pot.

His chief officer scoffed, "It looks like a play army, if sticks were swords and boys were men."

Our leader, Johannon, tried to respond calmly, "We are here to honor our fathers—" but was interrupted by the largest Rephaite.

"You damn dogs!" he thundered, his voice echoing throughout the valley. "What the hell are you doing here? Do you all want to die?"

The giant moved toward Johannon and the elders, only walking, yet covering ground with frightening, unnatural speed. In a mere breath, he was upon them. He slapped one man across the face, breaking his neck. A second he crushed with the butt-end of his spear, and we all heard the bones snapping. He lunged at another group; they scattered, but one wasn't fast enough. The unlucky man was lifted up like a small jar and shattered against the altar of stones gathered for the Lord.

At this, Johannon unsheathed a bronze sword—probably the only one possessed by my people in that camp—and charged the giant, crying out, "Away with you, you who are cursed by God!" Alas, such bravery deserved a better reward. The Rephaite met the challenger with his own iron sword, delivering such a crushing blow that Johannon's weapon splintered into a hundred pieces and his right arm hung lame.

As he stood there, dazed and helpless, the giant cleaved him in two, sending his upper half a dozen feet in the air and spraying those nearby with our hero's blood. Then he stomped his torso to paste, gnashing his teeth and cursing repeatedly as blood covered his legs like dye. At last he looked up and saw us all staring hopelessly. The Rephaite laughed at our weakness and cried out, "Run for your lives, or be sacrificed to Molech!"

At this, the Philistine soldiers broke from their ranks and charged, cutting us down to pieces. Chaos ensued. It was a bloody rout, with every man for himself. In the madness that followed, I was separated from my friends and carried away pell-mell by those who cared only for their own skin. As we rushed for higher ground, some of the younger boys were trampled. We poured into a rocky stream bed and up a steep, dry ravine, a dozen Philistines at our heels, slashing and stabbing upward at anyone who failed to push ahead of his brother. They were slowed only by the bodies they cut down, until we reached a height of forty or fifty feet, when several of us rallied and began heaving heavy stones down upon our attackers. We struck one in the crown, and he died. Another had his legs taken out from under him; he fell on his sword and tumbled back down the ravine. One of our pursuers was a young man with wide eyes. He had no beard and his armor hung loosely across his chest. He tried to catch a stone I threw, but it knocked him back and crushed his chin, and I heard the life gurgling out of him. The other Philistines retreated to gather reinforcements, and we jeered them and pelted them with rocks as far as we could throw.

As I said, this was an exceptionally narrow valley, not 100 feet across in places. Spurs and ridges extended from one side to the other like waves into a narrow harbor. We watched these Philistines run back to their leaders and point angrily at our position like tattletale children. However, the commander had few reserves to dispatch; his soldiers were spread out in wild pursuit across the valley and up the other side, too, which was neither as steep nor as high. The Israelites who reached the top entered a foot race with their attackers, and I believe most escaped.

In anticipation of a return of the swordsmen, I had gone about collecting heavy stones while the men around me climbed higher. I did not notice the approach of five archers to the base of our cliffs until they leveled their bows. Thus I found myself alone, the lowest and most tempting target of any Israelite. To my right there was a slight depression along a very slender ledge filled with nettles. Having no choice other than to serve as a Philistine needle cushion, I dove headlong into that most uncomfortable bed as arrows struck the cliff-side to my left and right. My arms and legs and face and neck were all stung with hundreds of the cursed plant's barbs, and I cried out in anguish. The archers surely assumed I was riddled with their darts. I lay low and did nothing more to persuade them otherwise, although the nettles continued stinging me mercilessly.

The rest of the Israelites dispersed across the steep slopes, every man finding cover as best he could under a hail of arrows. Some hid on bluffs or in crags; others burrowed in foxholes or buried themselves in the filth of a gulch that carved through the rugged cliffs. A few reached the crest and passed down the other side to safety, even as their brothers who climbed along-side them were pierced with arrows and fell to their deaths.

After this torment, three of the archers returned to the center of camp, but two were assigned to keep watch on the cliffs where we hid, and I dared not expose myself to their deadly aim. Quietly, I made a small stack of stones so I might peek safely over the ledge without drawing their attention. In the diminishing sunlight, I watched the Philistines execute the wounded, plunder the dead, and feast on our goat steaks and lamb.

Now, I suppose if their swordsmen had returned with the Rephaites, every Israelite on that cliffside would have been found out and run through. But from my vantage, the Philistines appeared to fear their allies; they kept their distance from the giants, who had no interest in the hunt. Indeed, they had no interest in food or loot either, or anything at all save inebriation.

Before the slaughter had ended, the three set to demolishing the altar to the Lord my people had constructed, and then commenced to seizing greedily every last one of our wineskins, stacking them high into a monument to their victory. Though it was dusk and I could not understand their mutterings, I could still see them well enough from their bonfires. It seemed they were establishing a consensus of order. Subsequently, they took turns consuming the wine, one gulping down an entire skin while the others glared jealously. When he finished, the next giant would take up his wineskin, never stopping for breath until the vessel was emptied. This continued past nightfall, round and round, without so much as a break to eat or piss, until each had consumed at least—*at least*—ten wineskins. In my years of rambling I have watched men suffering from the most extreme desert thirst, whose tongues had swollen after days without a drop of dew, demonstrate more restraint when they received water than these Rephaites showed for their murderous bounty, which must have measured out to well over a bath apiece.

And their fearsome voices! How they rose terribly with their drunkenness, echoing like lions' roars back and forth across the valley. They cursed the Hebrews first, then the Philistines, and last of all each other. The vulgarity of their threats was unimaginably cruel and crude, proving again not only the vile nature of their warped souls but also the corrupting influence of alcohol, which I have never suffered to taste.

The Philistines moved ever farther from the Rephaites, and I thought: surely these large ones will come to blows and rid the earth of their own wickedness. Indeed, I begged God it might be so. Suddenly, the smallest of the giants—who must still have been over nine feet tall—began vomiting like an Egyptian fountain. Every last drop he consumed was spewed onto the desert floor, and he collapsed in a heap to move no more. This delighted his companions, who laughed pitilessly like howling jackals celebrating a kill. I had hoped they might punish his intransigence by pinning him to the desert floor with their spears, but alas! They forgave his bluster and left him to sleep off the shame of his weakness. Carrying on as before, their hostilities intensified until the middle-sized giant stood up, reached for his sword, tripped, and fell backwards with a crash that shook Mahaneh Dan from end to end.

At last, the largest giant—the champion of the Philistines who had slain Johannon—consumed another three or four wineskins, stopping only reluctantly when he could no longer reliably deliver the spout to his lips. He lay down slowly, but rolled over on top of the remaining wineskins, causing the lot of them to burst with sharp "pops" beneath his enormous weight. This sound startled him up again, but he was dragged back down just as quickly by the heaviness of his own head, joining his comrades in deep sleep. This brought to a close the most profane, indulgent ritual I have ever witnessed. But their rasping drunken snores continued through the night, torturing the living, and perhaps even the dead.

Under cover of deep darkness, I crawled out of those damned nettles, but only just, and stared up into the stars until I drifted off, too. I alternated between dream and delirium, plagued by visions of deadly swordsmen, charging Rephaites, and a miserable, unquenchable thirst.

Chapter 5

When at first light of dawn deep shadows emerged from pitch darkness, Philistine "lumps" appeared scattered throughout the valley, sleeping peacefully among their smoldering fires. They were apparently well satisfied after a night of abundant feasting and thought themselves secure in their victory, for I spied no watch. I should have gouged out their eyes! But such an unmanly plan was repulsive to me in those days. Also, the Lord remembered mercy when he showed his servant a small trickle against the rocks behind me. Once I had satiated my thirst, my wits returned. As they say, "In the mount of the Lord it shall be seen."

The sky lightened to ominous red, and lo! Many of those "sleeping Philistines" were dead Israelites, lying in eerie, unnatural positions. What a bitter loss of beloved sons.

Staring down at this slaughter, I recognized Isnach splayed out among so many other broken bodies. The increasing light revealed his wavy yellow hair and striped tunic—the latter marked by a deep crimson stain—less than a stone's throw from the feet of the giants.

Now I faced a fierce dilemma: his family, our neighbors, had always treated me with sincere affection, and I grieved for their loss. His elderly father never failed to take an interest in my welfare, often going out of his way to share sweet bread and other treats when he asked about my affairs. Isnach was his pride and joy, and the two were exceedingly close. Though I have never been a sentimental man, it was intolerable that his only son should be left to bleach in the sun, or worse, thrown into Molech's bonfire, so his skull and bones could decorate one of the demon's shrines. I felt absolutely compelled to prevent that outcome and to return him to his parents, but… this was not so easily accomplished.

Isnach's body was lying among enemies bound to awaken shortly. Additionally, I was a Nazirite from birth among my people and forbidden by an oath to my God from touching any dead body, even blood relations.

Deliberating for a time how I might "have it both ways" and fulfill my present conviction without sacrificing my calling, I decided I could at least safely avoid any fleshly contact with Isnach by carefully wrapping him in one blanket with another. These were abundant in the camp since none of the Israelites had bothered to collect theirs in the rush to leave.

As for the Philistines and Rephaites? The longer I considered the danger, the more I convinced myself they should anticipate scavengers rummaging among the fallen. If they awoke, might they concede I was unarmed and intended no harm? Perhaps their bloodlust had been satiated last night.

Minutes passed and the sun began to brighten the mountains. Full daylight was near, and I felt my chances of success withering. Once the army awoke, they would assuredly not let me enter their camp. And if they became aware of my presence here on the hillside, spying on them as it were, they were just as likely to slay me as see me. Therefore, there was no value in further thought—the time had come to move.

With bated breath and racing heart, I put my trust in the Lord and snuck back down the hillside, neither disturbing stones nor snapping twigs. To reach my friend, I passed mutilated bodies that had begun to bloat, tiptoeing carefully between a group of sleeping Philistines on one side and the three snoring Rephaites on the other. I had just reached Isnach and begun wrapping him in one blanket, using another I double-folded as a buffer. In fact, I almost began to think I might safely escape when I heard a shout, and a guard came running over with sword drawn.

"Treachery, Philistines! To arms, to arms!" he cried. He was beating his sword against his copper shield, creating a racket that would have awakened the deepest sleeper in Sheol. "Who are you? Why are you here?" he screamed. "State your claim!" And he continued hitting his shield in the most irritating fashion. But there was fear in his voice. My reaching the middle of their camp left his life in as great a danger as mine. Philistines were sitting up, stupefied from sleep, searching for swords and shields, expecting raiders or slingers at any moment, but there was only me—alone, unarmed, with hands outstretched.

"Who are you?" the guard cried out again, continuing on loudly. "Why are you here? Assassin! Treachery, Philistines! To arms—"

I had not the chance to answer, for at that moment the chief Rephaite awakened, infuriated by the clanging. He sat bolt upright and struck the man such a blow that his armor crumpled, and I doubt he ever had the chance to doze off on guard duty again. My eyes met the giant's; he was as tall sitting as I was standing, and his face was hideous—massive in proportion, with pockmarked skin and sharp black eyes beset with pain.

"Who the hell are you?" he demanded, squinting and grinding his teeth.

"You slew this only son last night," I spoke up, shuddering as I pointed to Isnach. "I have come to return his body to his parents. Let them lay him to rest in the custom of our people before he begins to stink."

"Dagon be damned," he moaned, shaking his head slowly. "Take him and go," he ordered, rubbing his forehead. I continued wrapping Isnach, carefully, gingerly so as not to touch him, but the giant became dissatisfied with my progress. He shouted at me: "Dammit all to hell—just go away!" From his sitting position, he impatiently lifted Isnach and slammed him down onto the blanket I had carefully laid out. "Fire of Molech," he growled, grabbing his head and lying down again next to his companions, who moaned about their hangovers and insisted their chief shut up.

I showed no fear, but set about pulling Isnach to a tipped-over handcart that was only yesterday loaded with choice meats for the Israelites. It was nearer to the Philistines' section of camp, and they watched me groggily, uncertain how to respond. I told them, "The large one told me to leave. Best not make him angry like that other fellow," helpfully pointing to the Philistine guard who lay crumpled by the Rephaite's fist.

Carefully, I slid Isnach into the handcart by one blanket buffered against another, not allowing any contact between us, then stood the vehicle up and covered him. There was a general murmuring as I pushed the squeaky cart through the camp, but I refused to acknowledge whatever regrets the dazed Philistines felt for letting me escape, or to even look right or left or show any concern at all that might encourage their lingering thoughts of violence. They in turn did not want to antagonize their champions further, and kept their swords sheathed.

So I set out for Zorah on the main road, alone and unharmed—except for the bites of those damned nettles that covered me with red lumps.

Despite my escape, the Lord's judgment weighed heavily upon Israel. Had the sun not already been low in the sky when the slaughter began, few would have been left alive. As it was, more than 150 young men were killed, including 14 Danites. But it was Johannon's loss that was felt most bitterly among the tribes; he had no equal in arms or understanding of military matters, as I suspect the Philistines well knew. Worse still, many of those who saw his end were robbed of the will to fight. Without one to lead them, they returned to their homes and chose to endure any outrage, if only their own lives were preserved.

Chapter 6

All that morning I pushed Isnach along with great urgency, to ensure his parents could anoint their son before decay set in. Even as the distance between me and the slaughter at Mahaneh Dan grew, a nagging feeling persisted that I was being followed. Surely the Rephaites had continued sleeping off their drunkenness; therefore, I was convinced the Philistine commander disapproved of my escape and sent his assassins to remedy his regret. I was determined that my head not become another decoration on Gath's walls, and I collected stones to defend myself, only…whenever I checked over my shoulder, no pursuers ever presented themselves—not on the path behind me nor on the hills above.

By midmorning, my suspicions about this "tail" had grown extreme. I vowed to make my stand. God had delivered me from the Ephraimites, the Philistines, and the giants; surely, he would do so again.

I waited around a bend, ready to let fly my "quiver" of stones—and I was in truth a deadly aim. But who should appear but a runt of a boy. He had the look of an Edomite—with his exceedingly low hairline and unibrow—but the sour dog smell gave him away as a Philistine.

"Why do you pursue me?" I demanded.

He startled badly, not expecting confrontation, but he gathered himself and stepped forward. "You confronted Kabora Rachm." He paused, recognizing my perplexity: "The giant, Kabora Rachm! Don't you know he's killed 140 men?"

"The Israelites will be avenged, and the Danites avenged by two."

He made no reply, and we stood staring at each other. Eager to be on my way, I called to him again: "Return to Gath or wherever it is you call home and follow me no longer, because I am in a hurry to deliver this one to his parents before the stink sets in. At this time yesterday, I threw my own brothers off a bridge. How much less would I spare you."

"Please, let me come with you!" he cried, putting his hands out. "I have almonds and olives," and he held out a well-laden bag, taking steps closer.

The noon hour approached, and I had not eaten since before the carnage at Mahaneh Dan. A meal was suddenly a most welcome thought. I felt no fear of this small Philistine—Carillon was his name—and after some thought, agreed to his request. We walked on in silence until his bag of treats gave out.

Then I found my annoyance at this hanger-on renewed, so I asked again, "Look, why have you shared these choice morsels with me?"

He waited some time before answering, "Where do you live?"

"With my family and my people. What is that to you?"

Carillon sighed and said, "You spoke up to Kabora Rachm, yet even the Philistines tremble before him—and rightly so! He slew the guard before you. How is it you approached him without fear?"

"I made a vow to my God that if he would deliver me, I would gather this one to his parents," I said, gesturing to Isnach. "And as the Lord led, so I followed. Besides, your giant drank enough wine for a hundred men. He was not in a right frame of mind. Now again, what is all this to you?"

He continued to hesitate until I lost patience: "What is your secret mission? Are you a spy for the Philistines? Do you want this body for Dagon or Molech? I swear they will receive your blood first!" And I raised a fist.

"No! Stop!" he pleaded, cowering. "Listen, I will tell you. You said you would avenge the Israelites against Kabora Rachm. But did you know he has caused the Philistines grief, too? Of the 140 men he has killed—"

"I do not care about any Philistines. I hope you have been paid richly in suffering. You brought the tyranny of the Rephaim upon yourself. Your rulers treat those fallen ones as favored sons and sacrifice to Molech on their account."

"Yes, they are stronger, and the Seranim are indebted to them. Therefore, we cannot disobey them. But the Philistines do not love them. My father was murdered by Kabora Rachm for refusing to share my mother, and she and my sister were raped to death by the giant. So I, too, have taken a vow: to avenge my family. Yet I can do nothing. For when he appears like a temple pillar, my heart quivers, my knees wobble, and I vomit and faint. Yet you fear him not, though he adds up to more than two of you, tall as you are. How is that?"

"It is simple," I answered. "I am not a Philistine coward. The word of the Lord is my strength."

"That is no help to me, because we Philistines worship Dagon," Carillon said. "Perhaps the word of the Lord would invite you to challenge Kabora Rachm... Or if not, you might slit his throat. While he slept. While he was out of his mind with wine."

"Pha!" I answered. "You mistake me for a Philistine. A backstabber. A murderer."

"He who slays a Rephaite is no murderer. Even your own people say so! They pay the bounty—"

"I know what my people say. And no bounty is paid without the foreskin—"

"I've a knife. I could collect the foreskin."

"You could not hold the foreskin," I answered, taking his measure. "It would surely weigh more than you."

"I could too manage Kabora Rachm's foreskin!" Carillon argued. "Once you kill him, I could take the testicles, too—one to avenge my mother, the other for my sister. And if they proved too large, I could hire an ass."

"The testicles are unnecessary," I scowled. "And I have no doubt you would find a way to deliver the foreskin—and steal my reward."

"Never! For Kabora Rachm's life and the completion of my vow, I would most certainly return the foreskin to you."

"But I am a Nazirite," I protested. "I can touch no dead thing."

"Then I will carry the foreskin for you—all the way to your home!"

"I cannot have a foreskin in my home, for I am a Nazirite."

On and on we argued until at last I tired of his pique, for I was no assassin. I have been in many fights, but each was fair in its own right. Not once did I dig a pit for an adversary, nor did I fear anyone saying, "Aha!" to me.

Chapter 7

By the time Carillon and I arrived in Zorah, word had already spread about the disaster at Mahaneh Dan, and a dark cloud of mourning hung over the land. Those we passed on the highway would not consent to look me in the eyes—especially not when they saw my grim features or discerned my cargo. They just hurried along their way, keeping heads down and mouths shut. Not since the days of Abimelech and the destruction of Shechem had fear gripped the people's hearts like this.

As far as delivering Isnach to his family, I will not speak of it. It was one of the lowest moments of my life, and the sorrowful display pains me still.

When I arrived home, my Uncle Morson and Aunt Hama were visiting my parents, and they sat together lamenting this latest calamity, worrying in fear and dread for my safety. They cried out in sweet relief when I announced myself at the door, but the women began to wail when they saw me because I was red and swollen from my night in the nettles.

Despite carefully explaining the circumstances behind my appearance, the sisters were incredulous that I would "choose" such a hiding place. They brushed off my explanation that men who are running for their lives do not have the luxury of hunkering down on an ideally manicured lawn, and they found it inexplicable that "comfort" and "security" might be at odds. It is no wonder they make poor soldiers, and not just on account of their monthly uncleanness. When my uncle and father came to my defense, Aunt Hama argued belligerently that if she were still a young virgin, she would not lie down in a bed of nettles—not if all the Nephilim on earth were in pursuit—and wagered sight unseen she could find a better place to steal away on the mountainside.

In the days that followed, a strange thing happened. For my troubles recovering Isnach's body, the boy's parents sang my praises from the rooftop, and all Israel heard. From Shiloh to Lachish and the Dead Sea to the Great Sea, everyone was desperate for some good news and a reason to believe. It never occurred to me that my actions would give them the hope they craved. A rumor was born, and the rumor mill worked its course, and Israelites in all quarters began saying, "The young man Samson made demands of the Philistines, and even the Rephaim obliged to meet them."

Once I heard this silly tale, I decided it was close enough to the truth that I need not offer correction, though it may not have borne its weight before old Moses. I had been entirely unknown among my people; now, everyone began to speak well of me, and some foolishly claimed my "triumph" was a sign God still favored Israel. If that was true, I thought it ought to have been the Philistines collecting their sons from the valley floor.

For the next month, many important Danites came to pay tribute to my bravery on account of my service to Isnach's family, including Torgan with his parents. How relieved I was to see him alive. These visitors called me a true friend and a hero for all Israel. And when their wives laid eyes on me, as often as not, they burst into tears and kissed my head, saying, "Look at how he suffered for his friend!" After the impasse with my mother and Aunt Hama, I kept quiet about the source of my "injury," milking the attention for all it was worth—though what sort of enemy they thought could inflict a rash, I never did find out.

In spite of my emerging fame, not all was well. This was also the time that rascal Carillon beguiled my father into taking him on as a harvester, blubbering most shamefully about his own murdered father—as if that were any concern of ours. I had only intended to repay the almonds and olives I ate, so no Philistine could ever say he helped Samson, but now he was here to stay. All of this happened against my adamant protestations, which of course proved more than correct in the end. But my father had a particular lenience immune to reason for those he perceived as weak or unfortunate, and Carillon measured high on either standard. He was as pitiable as an orphaned lamb.

Somewhat surprisingly, he made himself useful during the grain harvest, toiling diligently from the first hour on, until I recanted my doubts and credited my father's hire. As the slaughter at Mahaneh Dan and my deeds regarding Isnach faded into memory, Carillon and I worked side by side into the summer, and I confess I began to find his company amusing. He spoke endlessly about women, a foreign subject to me in those days, and about his lust for them. Though he was younger, he was also more experienced. He had used a whore to ease his loneliness in the days following his family's destruction at the hands of Kabora Rachm, and his stories awoke in me a new curiosity for intimacy.

But as he captured my attention and friendship, so too did his productivity diminish, which I believe he understood. He countered my frustrations with increasingly boastful stories about any number of floozies. The more he spoke of breasts or beauty, the less he threshed and bundled. And if he had not been the sole source of conversation on such a fascinating subject, I would have beaten him all the way back to Gath, where he could have embraced his natural role as a contemptible beggar among a pitiless people.

One day he invited me to visit a certain Philistine prostitute. I refused, but he continued pestering me. "Look, Samson," he would say, putting his arm around me. "She is not the kind of woman you marry. You just sleep with her, then you leave. It's easy. I will even let you go first. She is just a whore, you know."

By chance, this was about the time we were harvesting lentils, an odious bean I always found disagreeable in taste and effect, whether in soup or bread. Carillon gorged on both, and the result was a continuously unbearable stream of flatulence. I did not need to defile myself with his Philistine whore—I was already thoroughly defiled by his putridity. Besides, his usefulness had diminished so sharply even my father grew tired of his excuses; he was not even gathering a basketful a day, and most of his energy went to complaining of a sore back or tender hands.

For those reasons, I felt no compunction when I warned him not to release air again in my presence, or else he would regret it until the end. At that very moment, he discharged such a sustained, foul-smelling fart—and laughed so hysterically—that I grabbed him by the neck and threw him into a pile of oxen filth that was gathered for the wheat fields.

"You find it so funny," I said. "This will entertain you until the great throne judgment."

Carillon was furious, though in truth his smell was much improved. He stormed off—never to return, I imagined, which would have been fine with me.

Much to everyone's surprise, he came back three weeks later, as we were collecting the earliest chickpeas. He humbled himself to my father and begged for a renewal of employment, promising tireless effort, and blaming his previous sluggishness on injuries now supposedly healed. He started crying again about his father and the surpassing difficulties he had endured throughout his life, as if death or poverty were unusual circumstances. Once more, my father granted his request over my protestations. And as before, Carillon started well enough, pinching off heaps of pods that compared favorably to our top men.

His newfound enthusiasm was decorated, as it were, in a similarly new red and blue tunic. Though he avoided me at first, he eventually reached out to apologize and make peace. I discovered his inspiration was a young Philistine woman in Timnah.

"I don't mind telling you, Samson, I have been making love to her." He spoke slowly, with a deep, satisfied sigh. "Her father pays me to watch his barns on the first and fourth nights of every week, and turns a blind eye to our activities— so long as we are discreet, I do my job, and she does not get pregnant."

Raising his unibrow slyly, he added, "You know, she has a *beautiful* sister."

Now he had my ear, though I feigned disinterest. I had not wanted any part of the whore he previously offered, but Carillon's description of *this* girl enflamed my curiosity. He promised she was just my type: well proportioned, but also prim and demure. Not only so, but she lived nearby—barely three miles away. In fact, from where we stood atop our property, the vineyards surrounding her father's valley estate were in plain view. We could easily visit upon completion of the day's labor and still return home before the end of the first watch. Then Carillon sweetened the offer further, saying Shealtah— for that was her name—did not care for Philistine men but was warm to Hebrews, especially anyone as handsome as I.

I denied him weakly, so Carillon continued pressing. After a little back and forth, I decided, "What could it hurt?" and conceded. That very night, we set out for Timnah.

Chapter 8

I pushed my hair back with olive oil, loaded a small wicker basket with our finest dried figs, and joined Carillon in nervous excitement. As I said, our footpath was little more than three miles, but it began to feel as if it might last a lifetime, such was my anticipation.

On the way, Carillon resumed his foul boasting, insisting he was blessed by the gods with unnatural prowess in bed, no woman could fail to be overcome with bliss by his lovemaking, Seranim Occily ought to contract him to satisfy the ongoing needs of the royal harem, on and on. Though I tried to ignore his bluster, it was so crass and vile that he just about persuaded me to a vow of chastity. At last, we came round a vineyard and saw clearly in the moonlight a two-story brick home atop a low rise, brightened with torches and surrounded by date palms.

We slunk past the embers of their fire; they had supped over that Philistine delicacy, seared jackal, for the whole courtyard smelled like dried piss. Carillon led me around back, where he gathered a few pebbles and threw them up at his lover's window, calling softly, "Schmealnah! Schmealnah!" After half a minute passed, he threw three more and called a little louder. The shutter cracked open and a coarse, ugly voice croaked, "In the name of Dagon, who is down there?"

"It's only me, Father—Carillon!" he squeaked. Clearing his throat, he added, "I came to see Schmealnah." With a quick look at me, he added, "I have some figs for her."

At this, he demanded my figs, but I refused. "You should have brought your own," I whispered.

"Hell, Carillon, you are not working tonight," the old man answered. "I know what you want. Give me the figs first."

Carillon gestured vehemently for my figs, but I held them at arm's length and whispered, "You came empty handed. Go collect your own!"

Then he cried out, "Do you want to meet Shealtah or not, Samson?"

"Who are you talking to?" the old man demanded.

"Only a friend—a rich Hebrew. He's here to speak with Shealtah," Carillon answered. "He has an offering of figs, too."

"Let's have them, young man. Don't be shy."

I conceded one, but Carillon responded loudly, "Do not be stingy, Samson!" Bitterly did I give up all but a handful, and these were passed up to the old man.

"Eh, decent," he said with mouth full. "Let me get my daughter for you, Carillon. I know she will be happy enough you are here."

We moved to the front door and waited. It was unbarred and pulled open, and lo! To my astonishment, an enormous girl appeared—just enormous. She was absolutely the fattest creature I ever saw. Her girth would have out-measured a two-story plumb line. Even now, miserable wretch though I am, remembering that heifer squeezing out the door—and imagining that pathetic waif Carillon mounting her!—is the only thing that still makes me laugh.

"Carillon, you scoundrel," I hissed. "I am going home; we already have livestock there."

"Hang on, Samson. This one is mine," he answered, leering intently at Schmealnah, who stood glowing in the torchlight like a fatted bullock. "Shealtah is still inside. Come here, Schmealnah, my queen, and meet my Hebrew friend Samson."

She waddled over and embraced Carillon, covering him with kisses, and he disappeared in her billowing robe. Grotesque slurping, smacking, and giggling followed, until she left him and came to me. She stroked my arm seductively, which I do not mind saying had no effect on me—none at all. She was garnished in jewelry and lace. There were rings on her ears and fingers, and her bead necklaces and bracelets rattled and chimed as she moved about.

When I pulled away, she asked flirtatiously, "Am I so horrible to you, Samson?"

If a woman put that question to me today, I would not hesitate to give her a fair answer. But in my youth, I was not so forthright, and I bit my tongue. If only I had been more honest, I may have been spared much misery.

"You have come for my older sister, Shealtah, I know," she said, smiling and running her fingers through my hair and down my shoulder and arm. I winced, but Schmealnah rolled her eyes playfully and sighed. "Oh, I am sure she will like you. You are very strong. She prefers foreign men anyway, as Carillon must have told you. But did he also tell you that Philistine men value larger women? Tell him, Carillon."

If that were true, she should have had her pick of wealthy suitors. Why, then, had she settled on Carillon, who must surely have been the least desirable male in all Philistia? I never found out, because Carillon desperately insisted she fetch Shealtah so the two of them could be alone.

Schmealnah disappeared back into the house, and I prepared to leave. "I have beheld the behemoth," I told Carillon bitterly. "Surely the tales are diminished. Let us return home—tomorrow will be an early rising."

"Samson, we just got here." He brushed me off. "Give Shealtah a chance. You have not yet seen her. You will like her, I promise. Tomorrow night, you will beg me to come back. Besides, Schmealnah is beautiful. She is not too big, you know."

"Carillon, she outranks the Nephilim. You should run for your life! Her breasts will crush you. She ought to be kept in a pen with the other—"

I stopped short when a maiden of unimaginable beauty exited the door, approached me boldly, and took my arm. "Let us walk, Samson, and give Carillon and Schmealnah their *privacy*." Shealtah sighed and then smiled hopefully. "I want to go with you."

Chapter 9

For glory and beauty! Shealtah was an angel, perfect in her womanly form. Indeed, her beauty must have been the only thing Carillon ever understated. In all my years in the company of women, I have never seen her equal, neither in Philistia or Israel, nor in Greece or Egypt.

Her long hair was black and fell playfully like a veil in front of one of her large, dark eyes, which sparkled even at night. At once charming and evasive, her wry smile belied an enduring frustration in her home. As a young man with no prior female companionship, I especially relished the outline of her bosoms. The sight of a woman's chest has been an enduring weakness ever since, but the Lord rebuked me when you Philistines tore out my eyes.

It is more than twenty years since Shealtah went the way of all the earth, yet somehow she still overpowers my mind— sweet and innocent, lovely and alluring, surpassing beauty beyond compare. She enraptured me with her touch and took ownership of my heart. There was never another like her, nor will there ever be. Though I was nervous on account of my inexperience with women, she put my heart at ease. In flickering torchlight, I was smitten beyond hope, and I do not doubt she knew it, too.

She led me to a veranda, and we sat side by side with arms touching. She inquired politely about my mother and father and about my siblings, but she did not pester me with inappropriate questions about land or boundary stones or crop yield, as do some women who are obsessed with wealth. Similarly, she told me briefly about her father and sister, mercifully sharing little about Schmealnah (any discussion of her would surely have snuffed out all romantic possibility). She vouched to the quality of her father's vineyards, which she thought would please me—though she did not know about my Nazirite vows, and for once I kept them to myself. In every way she enchanted me. She also delighted in the figs: "Oh, Samson, this one is so good, you must try it!" she would exclaim, or "I have never had a fig so good," as she coyly fed me the other half.

We talked easily for a time, until our conversation wound its course and I feared she was growing tired. Just before I offered to let her retire, she leaned over and kissed me. That was something entirely new, and it changed my life like a flash of lightning. Though we kissed, I did not have relations with her because I was determined to honor her, my parents, and her father. I also wished to ensure that no trouble would come upon her before we married, which I already had my heart set on. Yet in the end, she did not hold propriety or loyalty in the same regard, and I ought to have heeded the warning before it cost me everything…but, that portion of the story at the proper time.

I do not know how far the moon traversed before Shealtah and I were interrupted by Carillon and Schmealnah, who began to make an obnoxious racket on the pathway to our veranda. She had been drinking wine, had fallen, and Carillon was not strong enough to stand her up again. The two of them were laughing hysterically, and Shealtah stamped her foot and squeezed my hand in deep annoyance.

Shaking her head, she said her sister would be forced to roll back into the house unless we helped her up. And if we did not, Schmealnah would feign injury and demand to be waited upon in the ensuing days. Shealtah's life would be reduced to miserable servitude.

Thus, a pattern of interruption was established—one we never did escape. We went to them and righted Schmealnah, who was as helpless as a tortoise on its back. As we were into the second watch and he was satisfied, Carillon suggested we leave, and I reluctantly agreed. But before we did, Shealtah pulled me close and asked when I might visit again.

"Tomorrow," I whispered, "right after I speak with my parents about a dowry." She took a sharp breath, brushing the hair away from her eye and letting her hand run down her cheek and neck and across her shoulder.

She said, "Would you really rescue me from my sister?"

"Yes, I swear it will be so," I said, kissing her again. I promised her I would demand that my parents begin discussions with her father immediately. In truth, I could do no less. I was defenseless against her, and I would not have delayed a wedding for the Ark itself.

Though youth is gone, light has given way to darkness, joy has come to misery, and hope exists only in the grave, yet the memory of that first introduction to Shealtah remains sweet and uncorrupted. I was powerless to her touch, and I miss her still, in spite of what ensued.

Chapter 10

Yes, before I had occasion to visit Shealtah twice or to look at her face in the honest light of day once, before I kissed her goodbye that first night or took a single step away from her father's property, I made up my mind she would be my one and only lawfully wedded wife. You may think it odd a Hebrew of certain means would honorably pursue a Philistine, especially when it seemed the "dishonors" might be readily available if she was anything like her sister. But I was naïve and smitten, and determined to live without shame. I also wanted to secure the exclusivity of her love, which is never quite so sure a thing in Philistia.

There were obstacles to our marriage, of course. Shealtah's father, Dallim, was no fool, but a shrewd, successful cropper with an unbreakable commitment to his own rights. At the same time, my parents would need to bear up under scrutiny and scorn from our people, who do not approve of foreign women any more than you Philistines. However, there never was a wedding without dowries or disapproval, and I had no intention of breaking either tradition. Besides, our foremost prophet, Moses, chose a desert minx from a distant land to bear his children, yet our Lord spoke to him face to face! On what grounds should I be held to a different standard?

Leaving Shealtah that first night felt like a cold descent into Sheol, as it did every time I said goodbye before we married. Considering my only prior experience with the Philistines concluded with an unprovoked massacre, concern was justifiable, no? These fears, along with thoughts of engagement, social ostracism, and the impending carnal wonder that validated any measure of suffering, all spun together around my head like cream in a butter churn. At least this made it easier to ignore Carillon on the walk home, who had begun crowing about his "monumental" conquest as soon as we were out of earshot.

Eventually, he tired of bragging and sought gossip for his lover: "Samson, did you lay with Shealtah?"

I ought to have thrown him into a tar pit for such chutzpah. At the time, though, I felt indebted for the introduction, so I only smiled and shook my head slightly. But he read into that his own lusts, letting out a loud whoop. "I told Schmealnah you would have your way with her sister, but she said never— well, I cannot wait to tell her I was right!"

"Hush!" I growled, and then lightened my tone: "Look, I am not saying anything other than I enjoyed her company." I paused before adding, "*Very much.*" I have rarely resisted these sorts of self-indulgent comments, though they have never done me any good, least of all here. Carillon was so amused, he responded with gibberish.

"Oooo Samson," he teased. "You are a man now, you sweet bee! There is a new keeper of the hive, and you have taken all the honey!"

I had no idea what any of this innuendo meant, and I doubt he did, either—but he went on and on with his "poetry" until I could take no more: "Buzz off, Carillon! Dwell on your old milch cow, and stop fixating on my young lamb. I did not sleep with her." He sulked for a time, and muttered that Schmealnah was actually the *younger* sister, but we were nearly home and I was mercifully spared from any more of his buffoonery.

That next morning, I awoke only a little later than normal. My heart was burdened with unresolved love, and I dressed quickly to present demands to my parents.

They were discussing one thing or another over breakfast when I burst into their den. "Father, mother—" but he interrupted me.

"Samson, you look disheveled. It is not like you to sleep in. Are you ill?"

As I assured them of my good health, my mother slid a plate over. She said, "Here, have this slice of malted barley loaf to regain your strength before you go out with the workers."

I thanked them and hurriedly took a small bite to honor their goodwill. "Listen to me," I cried. "I have to speak with you about something important. I have seen a Philistine woman in Timnah."

"Timnah?" they said. "What were you doing there?"

I said I went with Carillon.

My father sputtered: "Carillon? The Philistine? I thought you wanted him sacked!"

"I have not said that since the lentil harvest."

"His work appeared strong for a time," my father drifted off, gazing out the window.

But my mother argued back, "Samson says he has not been so diligent lately."

"Is that true, Samson?" my father asked, snapping to attention again. "I thought he had gathered vetch well enough."

"Yes, he did well enough with the vetch, but the flax— look, this is not what I want to discuss," I said, shaking my head. "As I was saying, I saw a Philistine woman in Timnah last night—"

They interrupted again to say they had already heard that part.

I said, "Well, you have not heard this part. I want you to get that woman for me as my wife."

My father choked on his milk, causing the drink to erupt out his nose. My mother bore the brunt of this expulsion. As she wiped herself off, she asked with wounded voice, "Son, how can this be?"

"I am burning up on account of this woman, and I will settle for no other," I insisted, slapping the table for emphasis. "You must make the usual arrangements with her father. He is wealthy but can be reasoned with, and you need to prepare an acceptable dowry."

They looked like sheep that had borne the brunt of an overzealous shepherd's rod. Their mood worsened when I could not answer any questions about Shealtah's family—although I still do not understand why her mother's particular disposition, her father's male relatives, or the family's acreage should have any bearing on our marriage. Besides, it turned out her mother was mortally torn in labor with Schmealnah, an unfortunate but unsurprising result of the girl's corpulence. How one who bore beautiful Shealtah also conceived that prodigious hussy, I will never know, though it must have been a terrible disappointment.

My adamancy failed to persuade either of them, and we circled round and around our various impasses until my mother finally begged, "Isn't there an acceptable woman among your relatives or among *all* our people? What about your cousin Anna?" My father grimaced at the suggestion.

"Anna?" I shouted. "No! No now, and no forever! They do not call her 'Leah-Anna' for nothing." Seeing my mother's fierce offense on behalf of her niece, I said, "Look, I mean no harm, but she is plain and...not the sort that appeals to me."

My father huffed in agreement—which drew a withering look from my mother—but he was hardly on my side. "Must you really go to the uncircumcised Philistines to get a wife, Samson? Please, say it is not so," he begged.

"Look, I cannot tell you how little our relatives interest me," I said. "And it is no different for the rest of the Israelites.

Shealtah the Philistine, daughter of Dallim, is the one I love. Come now, get her for me. She is the right one for me."

My mother burst into tears, and I grabbed the malted barley bread and walked out to attend to my work. Before I left, I overheard my father say, "What can we do with this son of ours? Once his mind is made up, you cannot convince him any more than you can push an ox backwards."

I thought his criticism wrong on two accounts, and I turned to explain that I did once push an ox backwards into its pen after my younger brother mistakenly unhooked the gate latch. It was a battle of wills certainly, but the ox gave way once he understood I was the master.

However, this story only caused my father to dig in his heels further. He said I should have fixed a lead and returned the ox in a forward fashion, and besides, he and my mother both grew irritated with the subject and ordered me outside. Neither has ever received correction well. That added to the sting of their disapproval, which felt exceedingly harsh. Yet here, from this dungeon, I am confronted daily by my own folly, and am forced to concede they were at least in part correct. My very imprisonment testifies to their reproach.

Still, though my sin found me out, what man can plead innocence regarding women? We are all guilty from Adam.

Chapter 11

During the season that followed, my insistence on wedlock was countered repeatedly with steadfast hesitation on the part of my parents, who only reluctantly pursued a correspondence with Dallim when their deep well of excuses ran dry. Until then, complaints directed at their lack of progress were waved off, with no small measure of irritation. "These things must be arranged properly, Samson," my mother often said. If I had a silver coin for every excuse housed in "propriety," I believe the Lord God Almighty himself might consider an offering for a new pair of eyes. Still, the waiting was not without use: It gave me ample space to reflect on our patriarch Jacob, who it is said worked a week of years and a week besides until he received the bride of his desires, yet he found only the last seven days burdensome, such was his love for her.

After several increasingly contentious letters between my father and Dallim—all masked in the sort of false deference the Philistines require—the time came for a decisive meeting, and my parents made preparations to visit the old rascal.

When they left, the grape harvest was nearly complete; I was to follow once the gathering was finished, the fruit stored or shipped, and the workers paid. Without my father's soft touch to protect them, I pressed the hands on like a cruel taskmaster from dawn's first light until sun's final flare. So eager to be on my way was I that I filled twice as many wicker baskets as the next best man. The morning we finished, I distributed their shekels fairly, dividing my own pay between the most valuable pickers to ease any sore feelings. Needless to say, Carillon received no additional reward, though he complained most bitterly when he was passed over, arguing he "thought we were friends" and wondering if he should "take his wares elsewhere." Through many years of overseeing labor, I have come to understand it is almost always the laziest and least valuable who cry the loudest over the "injustice" of their agreed upon compensation. This was doubly true of that lazy-bones, though I am glad to say he found no sympathy among his coworkers. If he had "earned" a single extra shaving of copper, not even Pharaoh's pyramids could have held the gold I would have owed the others, including the women.

Most of the grapes were sent away to my Uncle Morson, who had a thriving winery estate, and once that business was settled, I hurriedly bathed, put on my best tunic, and set out for Dallim's home.

It was exceedingly hot, and the land was parched from a long spell without rain. You might have tracked me all the way to Timnah for the dust I raised in my hurry to join Shealtah. There was no other cloud in the sky.

I was more than halfway there, coming round the switch-back where the foothills descend into the Valley of Sorek and Judah's path runs alongside the Ramah streambed, when I sensed an uncomfortable stillness—no birds singing, and even the cicadas quieted. I ducked under a gnarled old oak that twisted low across the path, but before I left its canopy, I felt the hair on my neck stand up. Turning back, I saw a huge male lion wedged in the base of the tree's crown, in the crotch where the trunk splits into two main stems. He was eyeing me lustily, and his tail swayed haphazardly like a barn cat readying to pounce on a rat. We looked at each other, that lion and I, until his claws unsheathed, his lips flared and teeth bared, and he lunged at me with a deafening roar.

As he flew through the air, I thought of Shealtah, my family, and the life I had planned. I had various recollections of childhood and other experiences, too, all rolling out together in a record of sweetest memories. They passed through my mind like a flash of lightning, before the hunter had scarcely left his branch, and I held each one dear. Anger swept over me, and I determined he would not make a meal out of me. Remembering a "shepherd without a flock never outran a lion," and not being in possession of any scapegoat, I had but one option: I gave my own full-throated yell and sprung to meet that golden devil in the air, landing my elbow square into his soft nose. He yowled in surprise as we fell in a heap; I had the better of the landing, too, and wound up on top, so I clubbed his chin shut with my other elbow. This had less of an effect than I hoped, for it drew little blood from his mouth, and worse, allowed him to sink a heavy claw into my shoulder. Over and over we rolled deep into the brush beside the path until I pushed away and jumped back; he flipped to his feet, too, but I was the quicker and delivered a kick with a two-step start to his stomach that would have miscarried leviathan. I heard his air exhale as he flew into a crag, and though I also fell from the impact, here I believe he understood his doom. Growling and hissing, the lion tried to escape up the hillside, but I pulled him down by the tail, collecting a heavy stone in my other hand as I did. When he snapped at me, I crushed his head. And when he collapsed, I put my foot on his throat and pulled his front leg apart until I heard tendons snap away from the socket. He lay there whimpering, trying pathetically to slink away, his mane covered in blood.

Unexpectedly, I felt compassion at the sight of this doomed foe. So I granted him the same quarter he would have given me: I rung his neck and ended his suffering.

Stunned at this turn of events, I took self-inventory and was amazed when I found nothing more than the gash in my shoulder, which stung a little. Other than that and a well-dusted tunic, I was no worse for the wear, and I would wager most people who have tussled with a lion wish they could say as much. Brushing myself off and praising God for my victory, I continued on my way and arrived at Shealtah's without any further excitement.

Chapter 12

Bursting through Dallim's door, I shouted as I came up his stairs to the main room, "Mother! Father! I have conquered—"

They shushed me impatiently. There was a tense, awkward spirit of mistrust in the room, and my mother said crossly, "Samson, please, not now. We will discuss the harvest later." She motioned me to leave. Not one of them bothered to look at me.

I tried again: "The grapes were not—"

"Enough about the grapes, young man," my father said sharply, snapping his fingers and pointing me out of the room.

Here I was with the most unexpected victory since Jael nailed Sisera to the floor with a tent peg, yet no one would hear it.

"But look at my shoulder!" I cried.

They all turned and stared. Most of the blood was scabbed over and covered in dirt, or else hidden behind shredded shirtsleeve. The wound did not appear particularly dangerous to anything other than Dallim's white couches. He also made his annoyance plain, adding insult to injury when he called for his daughter: "Shealtah! Come and clean up Samson; he has tripped and dirtied himself." This I denied, but my mother spoke over me again, complaining I had ruined my best clothing through carelessness. When she finished, my father lectured I had better learn to be less clumsy before I had children.

Shealtah entered the room a moment later with a pitcher of water. "Oh, clumsy Samson," she teased, chiding me for my fierce scowl. She slipped a towel under my arm, took a ladle, and dribbled cool water over my wound, then dabbed blood and dirt gently away. She prepared a poultice of aloe and cinnamon, which I let her apply, though it was unnecessary.

My countenance lifted at her gentle touch, and my parents resumed their negotiations with Dallim.

Shealtah whispered to me, "Is this not exciting? Finally our parents meet. I began to fear they disapproved so strongly you would be forced to revoke your pledge. Or," she added with mock disapproval, "that you had found another to embrace."

"Never," I said. "Never to either. You are my choice, and you only I will have."

She blushed and smiled, but as we listened further, it became clear Dallim was driving a hard bargain. He believed his standing among the Philistines would be endangered by marrying off his firstborn daughter to a Hebrew—a fear my parents understood in their own right—and demanded a very considerable dowry to secure his position.

"Your son, he mentioned grapes," I heard Dallim say. "Tell me more about yields."

"You cannot add grapes to the contract, Dallim," my father shot back.

"Pomegranates, pistachios, and figs. Dates in return. These were the terms," my mother said, shaking her head.

"You did not say you had grapes," Dallim replied, wagging his finger at them. "Your son does not eat them, no?" After a moment his demeanor lightened like a man who has found a gold coin. "You know I have olives. We could work it out."

"Green or black?" my father asked.

"Green."

"I do not like green olives, and we are well supplied in oil anyway. But," he sighed, "I could consider adding almonds in exchange for—"

"What is the point!" my mother cried out. "Already we have been here for two days, and all the careful agreements have been changed a dozen times over."

I could take no more. I shouted at them all: "This is why I told you from the beginning you should have come straight here. I told you not to send letters, but no, you insis—"

"Quiet, Samson!" my father snapped. "You do not understand these things yet. Not until you have a headstrong son of your own." He took a deep breath and looked back at Dallim, counting something off on his fingers as he continued: "I can exchange five—*five!*—measures of almonds for..."

On and on they went, round and round, adding this, revoking that, like two merchants haggling for a final jar of oil in a seven-cor exchange.

Meanwhile, the dogs the family kept in a pen outside had begun barking uncontrollably. As it turned out, Schmealnah was slaughtering one from the pack. We discovered this a short time later when the vile smells of burning fur and offal invaded Dallim's home. He lit incense to mask the odor, but the differing scents mixed cruelly together, increasing greatly the unpleasantness of the setting.

Now, let me quickly interrupt this portion of the story to tell you another—like none you have ever heard before. Dallim had on his property a tame baboon, the only one I ever saw outside of Egypt. He traded for the beast from a caravan of Ishmaelites on the road from Thebes to Carchemish, the traders having promised it was genuinely trained by Egyptian harvesters to climb palms and retrieve date clusters. With an eye on reducing salary expenses, Dallim named the brute Pharaoh Ramesses, after that great antagonist of the Philistines, and set it to work.

For a time, the animal lived up to expectations, gathering more dates than the rest of the workers combined. But eventually, the baboon grew older and wiser and began to regret its toil for Dallim's profit. It had a taste for dates, too, but never received its fair share, only one or two from a cluster of hundreds. Souring on this arrangement, the baboon took it upon itself to renegotiate terms, consuming dates at the top of the tree to its satisfaction before returning the leftovers for the harvest.

To save his profits, Dallim began to cultivate the animal's taste for cake, which he reasoned would satiate its large appetite before its labor. Knowing full well the higher value of dates, he portioned out cake to excess just to be safe. But if the baboon at first appeared appreciative, its insolence soon grew further; it took airs and became entitled, demanding cake to go up a palm and the promise of cake in plain sight to come back down. Dallim obliged for a time, until the animal gathered upon its midsection such girth that it struggled and puffed its way up, and could return only a single cluster before requiring a long rest.

Recognizing the game was up, Dallim chained the animal and charged curious onlookers a coin for a view. Once visitors ceased, he had not the heart to discard Pharaoh Ramesses, because he had taken a liking to it in spite of its selfishness and felt partly responsible for its engorged state. Without shelter, it would surely have become a meal for jackals or lions in short order—or perhaps starved to death as a cake beggar. Either way, Dallim allowed the baboon to live a life of ease on his land, going here or there as it pleased.

And now, to return to the prior story. At that very moment, with negotiations underway, tensions high, and the stench of burned dog and incense wafting through the room, Pharaoh Ramesses entered our presence. My mother screamed and my father was alarmed, but the fat baboon paid them no heed. Like a man with a crutch, it put its hands on the ground and swung its short legs forward, loping about in search of food. When it found none, it went to Dallim to beg. Man gave beast one treat or another and scratched its neck, which caused the animal to grunt and groan in delight, much to our revulsion. Dallim continued talking as if this scene were not unusual.

My parents were still in a high state of alarm, but when they asked nervously about the animal, Dallim merely said, "This is Pharaoh Ramesses," without further explanation. Indeed, that was about the time I heard him offer to "sweeten the deal with lentils." I remembered the bean's effect on Carillon and looked at the angel who had bandaged my arm so delicately. "No lentils!" I cried out, jumping up. Everyone stared until I said, "Does not anyone want to know how this—"

Again, my father cut me off. "Samson, for the last time, stop interrupting. We are here for you! And do not draw any more attention to your filthy appearance. Either bathe or attend to Shealtah before we leave."

I never did tell them about my fight with the lion. I had hoped my victory would restore my parents' pride in me, which was reduced considerably ever since I made known my choice for a helpmate. Nevertheless, this unexpected secret played a decisive role in my tale, which I shall share soon enough. For now, I wandered off with Shealtah, assuring her all would work out between our families. We shared sweet dreams of the future, and caressed.

Chapter 13

Back on our property, this was the year our orchards produced the best harvest of my life—a good omen for my marriage as far as I was concerned. We were knee deep in pistachios, dates, and many other valuable crops, but Dallim used all this to his advantage, causing my parents continual grief while they negotiated. One night, I overheard my father reporting some of this back-and-forth deliberation to my mother. They were in the kitchen, dipping their bread into olive oil. She was irate.

"The almonds are Dallim's number one priority," my father was saying.

"But he said the dark grapes were most valuable to him," she answered. "And then light grapes, and then pomegranates."

"Yes, grapes of all colors for winemaking, then pomegranates and almonds. Almonds are his third number one priority."

"Third number one!" she said, shaking her head in exasperation. "This is the problem. Every day he haggles anew over what was decided yesterday. I have never known such a haggler!"

"Yes, he does haggle," my father agreed.

"He pushes too far, but then he rolls out the olives. Always the olives. Well, we don't want any olives. We have done fine without olives! But it comes to nothing anyway, because he tilts the table and they all roll away again. 'Of course I must take back the olives,' he says. I tell you, it is just too much."

My father said nothing, but stared hard into the oil, swirling his bread round and round. I cleared my throat and sat beside them, cutting my own piece from the loaf. "Why do you not just give him your final offer and force him to accept?" I asked. "He will not get a better one from his own people."

My father kept staring into the oil and swirling it. After an uncomfortable silence, he looked up at me and sighed deeply: "Because we were already given your final offer and forced to accept."

"What is the difference over a couple of hins of nuts?" I said.

"Really, Samson," my mother cried, "it's not a matter of hins or omers but cors and homers!"

"This is a year of abundance," I said. "Is it really too much?"

That is when my father explained Dallim had insisted on percentages of yields this year, to be matched in weight the following three years. "So you see," he said, "he uses a bumper crop against us, to secure a bounty that may never exist. He perceives your passion for his daughter, Samson, and trusts your will should prevail here. But God, who chooses one year to provide abundance, does also assign scarcity to others."

Dallim, you old villain! You were as crafty as a fox, but in the end you misjudged badly. The man thought he was trading away a discontented daughter for a windfall. My parents asked me to delay my marriage a year in expectation of a more routine harvest. I promised to make whatever recompense necessary to secure their obligations, only I would not delay my wedding. My mother pushed for a number of other concessions that would have better secured our interests, but in the end my father balanced out our conflicting demands as best he could.

Now, I do regret I was not more sympathetic to their concerns. They agreed to a disadvantageous exchange of product that may have cost them dearly had events unfolded differently. And yet, they sacrificed a great deal more before Shealtah and I united hands.

Chapter 14

Given the busyness of the late summer harvest, I attended my bride-to-be infrequently, and usually in secret because I did not want to encourage Dallim to raise his demands—but also because Carillon had a disagreeable habit of inviting himself along. This in spite of the fact that Schmealnah had tired of him considerably; he came home on more than one occasion cross and despondent from rejection.

As word got out about my impending nuptials, the same rumor mill that raised my profile after the crisis at Mahaneh Dan now leveled out any excess goodwill. My family was shunned by many of our neighbors in Zorah and the surrounding areas, though that included none of our business partners. "Sins of the son" notwithstanding, they knew my parents were honest to a fault, even when held in contempt. My father mostly brushed off these insults as storm clouds on the horizon, but my mother was troubled on many occasions. She was shunned at gatherings, shunned at the market, shunned at her weekly pottery confab. "I do not understand why things have to be this way," she lamented. Yet in truth she disliked many of these "shunners," which I reminded her.

"You complain on every occasion about these backbiting fussbudgets," I said. "*You* should shun *them*." But she raised her eyebrows at me, and I was shunned myself until her annoyance passed. My father took her side in spite of my arguments, just as always. I will never understand why a woman counts it loss when she is forced out of company she would rather avoid anyway.

Yet for all their protestations, conflictions, and frustrations, my parents nevertheless devoted generous thought and effort to the dowry to ensure my wishes were fulfilled. And they worked vigorously with a number of merchants to provide exceedingly more meat, beer, and wine for the wedding than Dallim required to ensure their hospitality was never questioned, nor could it be.

But when at last the arrangements were all agreed upon, the harvest was over, the Feast of Booths celebrated, and the winter rains come and gone—indeed, when every conceivable arrangement was completed *properly* (as they say) and the wedding less than a month away—that was when the publicans from Gath arrived.

They came with a hundred armed brigands and a handful of torchbearers who deployed immediately alongside our home, the servants' quarters, and our barn. Their commander asked if we would concede peacefully, and, taking our silence as affirmation, set his men to loading their wagons with the fruits of our labor—nuts, pomegranates, grains, and every last sycamore fig. Once the exaction was complete, these ruffians beat the hands with the flats of their swords and provoked the women obscenely. I would have gladly given my life to pummel just one of them, but I could see no way of doing that without forfeiting my family's lives and property as well. My brothers were still children—my mother had not weaned the youngest—and the torchbearers would have reduced everything to ash. Therefore, I bit my tongue and endured the shame of submission.

I was especially incensed that Carillon said nothing in our defense, but rather groveled from his knees hysterically like a woman for his own skin, repeating again and again, "But I am a Philistine!"

The commander of the Philistines kicked him across the jaw anyway, demanding, "What are you doing here then?" That was the first and only time I ever envied a Philistine officer.

After laying Carillon down, that same man warned my father of hard days to come. He said Gath faced pressure from Egypt in the south and Assyria in the north, and must either make trade or war. Since Seranim Occily had chosen the former, all surrounding estates must pay their fair share to secure peace. He assured us Asshur would not be so generous, while Pharaoh's hordes would ransack like a plague of locusts, sparing nothing but the vermin. This was a lot of bluster, which my father well understood; he bitterly urged the commander to at least leave enough for the vermin and to hold back the burners, or there would be nothing to plunder next year.

That rogue made it seem like a favor he was only pilfering a portion of certain crops. "This is not plunder," he said. "It is the price of safety, and a damn good value at that. You have not paid more than your fair share. Should you really live under the protection of the Philistines while others carry the load?"

I vowed then and there this man would "carry the load" for his villainy, and that vow I fulfilled in short order, as will be told—but not yet. His time was not at hand. His sin had not reached its full measure.

When he was satisfied with the amount of loot seized, he called for the torchbearers to retreat from the premises. One of those careless oafs allowed his fire to lick a broken branch hanging from our carob tree; I leapt to tear it down but was too late. In a mere breath, the leaves ignited, the fire arose, and the entire tree was consumed in a blaze. It spread rapidly to our small granary and the adjoining threshing floor, where chaff littered across the stones carried sparks straightaway to the remaining barley sheaves. These erupted in violent flames that rose as high as the top of the carob—that is, before the crown collapsed.

My father and mother cried out, "Why are you burning us out? We fulfilled your demands!"

The Philistine commander did not so much as turn to look, shooing them away as he walked off: "What are you still bothering me for? Hurry and douse the flames before you suffer greater misfortune."

We rushed to contain the fire—pulling away brush and beating the outlying flames with saturated blankets. The pathway around the threshing floor was rocky and well trampled by oxen, and our well was nearby, so the fire did not easily spread. Moreover, by God's grace there was no breeze that day, or else all may have been lost. In little time, the flames reduced the tree and granary to ash, and the fire mercifully died.

Yes, somehow that day might have ended far worse, though the damage in sum was severe, amounting to nearly a third of the value of that season's harvest.

Needless to say, we were not the only family to suffer. Weeks later, elders from the various tribes met to discuss these crimes. The Philistines had previously limited their "official" thievery to highway or market robbery, which was no small thing. If Seranim Occily now had his eyes on private homes and pantries as a steady source of plunder, this represented a considerable escalation of harassment.

Even still, the disaster at Mahenah Dan was fresh in everyone's mind. No one had the heart to confront the Philistines with their iron weapons; rather, they feared a further doling out of punishment. Such outrages were commonplace in those days, before the reckoning at Lehi. Not unless Shiloh itself was threatened would the Israelites have risked raising an army, and it would have been a poorly equipped one at that.

When those cursed looters left, my father asked if I would at last reconsider marrying a Philistine. Of course I denied him angrily. What fault of Shealtah's was this? The wedding was mere weeks away. Besides, I still thought I could disentangle her from her people—and make them pay.

Chapter 15

In the days that followed, I worked frantically to pick up the pieces around our property, to care tenderly for those servants left bruised and battered by the Philistines, and to comfort my family in their grief. Also, I was single-minded that we should still depart for my wedding at the appointed time, and I opposed all suggestions of delay. There was an unspoken insinuation throughout the household the ransacking was my fault since I was marrying a Philistine. To appease my mother and father, I swore an oath that I would gain vengeance on those responsible.

My father answered, "Samson, it is the Lord's vengeance that made the Philistines rulers over us. You ought to choose your words more carefully lest you call down judgment on yourself."

I said, "What I have said, I have said. God will vindicate me as he wills—you shall see."

"That is what I am afraid of," he said.

I tried a change in tone. "When I am married to Shealtah, Dallim can exert influence with the Philistines. Most of his product goes to Gath. They will not want to upset him. He will help us."

"Do you really think the Philistine rulers have any regard for Dallim's opinions?" my father asked. "I do not think they do. But if they do, which I do not believe, I still doubt Dallim will risk his standing for us."

"Perhaps not for us, but for his daughter and grandchildren."

He looked skeptical. Then he sighed and said, "If the Lord wills."

I avoided any further debate, setting my mind solely on the rapid restoration of order in our barn and across our groves. A careful accounting confirmed the Philistines had taken what amounted to a triple tithe out of our stores. After several weeks of ceaseless toil, we raised up a new granary, albeit more modest than the original. Of course, our distress was not only in the measurable loss, but even more so in the immeasurable shame of impotence against what was in truth a small gang of ruffians. Such weakness anguished every heart in Israel, but these sorts of seizures were increasingly common following the slaughter at Mahaneh Dan.

Under that cloud of grief, we nevertheless set out for Dallim's home at the appointed time—me, my mother and father, Uncle Morson and Aunt Hama, and that interloper Carillon, who half-persuaded my parents it would be valuable to have a "trusted" Philistine around since his people were not disposed to Hebrews. The latter was true enough, though his offer was not made with any sincere goodwill, but rather a latent desire for drinking and feasting gratis. Indeed, he not only proved useless in countering the subterfuge that came, but actually made it far worse.

Like Father Abraham leaving for a land he did not know, our small caravan departed with varying degrees of uncertainty, regret, and resolve. I was the only one eager, and this of course for the consummation of my marriage. We left in late morning, and by midday descended the hills along the Ramah streamed where I had overpowered the lion.

I suggested the women and Carillon rest. As they gathered their breath, I quietly stepped off the path and through brush to a small out-of-the-way bed of sorrel where the hunter's carcass lay. His innards were consumed, his flesh baked to leather, and the empty space in his ribs was inhabited by bees. Thinking only of my hunger, I pulled loose hide from the lion's neck and opened the honey chamber, scooping out several handfuls. I also filled a cup for my parents and my aunt and uncle. When I returned to them, they received the gift gratefully. Carillon was upset I had none for him, but I told him the bees had begun to swarm, and any more honey would come at a severe personal cost. He was too cowardly to check for himself.

As we walked along and I lapped up honey under the jealous glare of Carillon, I felt a certain measure of remorse for neglecting my Nazarite vows and dirtying my hands with the dead lion. Such an error in judgment was not a good omen for my marriage, but at the time, I thought the bountiful harvest back home was still the stronger of the two signs.

In the meantime, Carillon struck up a conversation with Hama, asking if she heard the story of how he and I met and how he shared his tree nuts without any expectation of repayment. She silenced him with a series of yawns that left him sulking twenty feet behind our party.

When we came into view of Dallim's estate, I was dismayed by a significant hustle and bustle of human activity upon his small hill. I knew my mother had sent ahead many animals for slaughter, viz. lamb, goats, quail, baskets of carp and catfish, which were tremendously difficult to secure, plus a half homer of wheat and two cors of wine. These, along with fruit and more grain from our estate and a number of silver coins, were intended to provide abundantly for the wedding party. But the *true* abundance was to be found in the number of Philistines lining up for free meals; Carillon was not the only hanger-on.

Outside the home, we passed two long tables of Philistine men set up underneath blooming almond trees. Though it was far from evening, they were all excessively drunk. One of them recognized me as the groom, and he led the party in loud cheers. "Sam-son, Sam-son, man of the hour!" they shouted, raising their mugs to me and drinking lustily. There must have been more than fifty! One excessively large fellow stood and bowed grandly, twirling his hands and welcoming us in the name of the great and beneficent god of the mighty Philistines, Dagon.

Do you know who this man was? Here is a hint: His robe was red and black, and he wore a necklace with many crystals and jewels. He had on his turban a large shark's jaw with rows of sharp teeth. With his long drooping mustache and his wide-set eyes, his face was reminiscent of a catfish.

Yes, this was my first meeting with Maruck, the very priest you Philistines assigned to administer my blood oath for this testimony. He was like a cinder in my eye, and it grieved me that when I was free, he forever eluded my hand. But what I failed to achieve, the Lord saw fit to complete when he demanded the man's life before I began this story.

Of course, no disagreements existed between us at that time. Even still, as he drew near, I was tempted to "throw him back again" across the table like an unwanted catch, though I settled for grunting at his greeting and entering Dallim's home (and he was too drunk to be insulted). It was fresh-smelling inside—the animals had all been moved out of the stables and the stalls cleaned and covered with fresh straw and pine boughs for the guests.

"Dallim, who are all these Philistines?" my father demanded. "A reception of this size was not a part of our agreement! There is not enough food to feed so many mouths—"

"There will be enough!" Dallim snapped. There was fear in his voice, and he added, "Maruck will control them—the large one with the jawbone, a holy man—he will send some of them away. But not all, or we will have much trouble and no wedding, for these fellows intend to seize what they can.

"Besides, I have offered these ruffians two barrels of beer—
out of my own purse!" he cried angrily at my father. Calming
himself, he took on a queer, distant look in his eye and stuffed
two dates into his mouth. As he chewed, he spoke: "When
the Philistines discovered the arrangements, they chose a large
wedding party for Samson, as is our custom," he said, spitting
one of the pits across the room into the bedpan. He sucked
the meat off the other slowly and deliberately. Pointing up to
a clay bird hanging from his ceiling, he continued: "Let your
worries be like the rook, who, though he pecks at your eyes
in the morning, eats the locusts from your field in the afternoon." He spat the other pit into the bedpan, too.

Hama was the first to speak: "An army of vagrants invades
your feast, and he talks about birds."

My father was equally dissatisfied by Dallim's proverb.
"We do not have time to discuss birds, Dallim! That Maruck
fellow—"

"Dammit, Manoah!" Dallim cried. "Don't you think I
know we are on a knife's edge? I should never have agreed to
this wedding. Never! The Philistines will gut me for giving my
daughter to a Hebrew—"

They began to argue, and I felt my wedding slipping away.

As their tones sharpened, I roared "Stop!" and slammed
my fist down on a small end table. It shattered under the force,
sending a bowl of mandrakes flying across the room. I had not
meant to break it, but the effect was exactly as I desired; the
room silenced, and they all looked at me with fear.

"Father, Mother," I said, firmly but respectfully, "the
wedding will go on. Those Philistines showed no hostility;
they are satiated with drink." With a resolved nod to Dallim, I
continued, "The food will be sufficient, and the party outside
will be reduced. There's nothing else to it. We will make due,
and"—with another nod to my parents—"I will find a way to

cover any expenses that run beyond your generosity." In truth, I had already begun to think how I might make the Philistines pay.

"Now," I said, "get me my wife, I want to lay with her!"

"His wife will not want to get in bed with new debts, that is for certain," Hama lectured, gathering the mandrakes from around the room.

I rolled my eyes, but my mother answered with a mother's understanding: "Samson's mind is made up, and he will not change it," she said, giving me a look that was both stern and tender. "He will do what is right."

"Father," I said, turning to Dallim, "let us go and rid ourselves of whatever of these loafers we might be rid of."

Chapter 16

I followed Dallim back downstairs to his front yard; he approached the priest Maruck meekly, apologizing profusely and groveling pathetically *in his own home* that the number of Philistines must be sharply reduced lest his reputation for hospitality suffer irreparable harm, for no one would have more than a bite to eat with so many mouths to feed.

To my surprise, Maruck agreed easily enough. He made a general announcement to the party that those who were neither invited nor friends of the family ought to shove off. There was hemming and hawing, but no takers. To show he meant business, Maruck began walking around the tables saying he regretted he should be forced to extend disinvitations. One by one, he picked up the poorest of the Philistines by the neck or ear, kicked them in the backside or slapped them with his metal scepter, cursing them: "Be away, you lazy freeloader!" "Get out of here, you ugly son of a whore!" "Who invited you, you dog-faced bastard!" until he had diminished their numbers by ten or twelve, at which time another fifteen or twenty excused themselves sheepishly, some remembering appointments and others complaining of excessive fatigue. One drunkard claimed he could not bear another sip of alcohol, as drink had a most debilitating effect on him, and he would not want to diminish the joy of others by his unfortunate sobriety.

This reduced their numbers to thirty, and Maruck said everyone else there was *his* personal guest. He could not ask anyone to leave without risking *his* reputation for hospitality. This was a smart move; it created a certain debt of friendship among those chosen to stay. And with that, Maruck made himself the master of ceremonies. Dallim was relegated to affable host.

Meanwhile, my father and mother had taken Uncle Morson and Aunt Hama to meet Shealtah—she waited on the rooftop with Schmealnah for our consummation. That gave me a few additional moments alone with these drunkards, and a more contemptible lot I never did see. They were busy entertaining themselves with boastful stories about their wives and lovers, Maruck the loudest of all. I doubt a single one knew Dallim or cared for my wedding. They were there for the party, for the food and drink. Even that mouse Carillon had already settled in with a large mug of beer. *Trusted Philistine*—pha!

For his part, Maruck said the Philistines were eager enough to have me as a brother, and I lied and said my people were just as determined to make Shealtah one of their own. Maruck asked if there was any other news from Israel—I think he was alluding to the ransacking his lord, Seranim Occily, had ordered. But I refused to give him the satisfaction of our family's pain, though I am sure Carillon told all.

Knowing how they were already well emboldened with drink, and understanding well enough the Philistines' greed for tall tales and teasers, I said, "Have you any interest in a wager? I have invented a new riddle. If you can give me the answer within the seven days of the feast, I will give you thirty linen garments and thirty sets of clothes—one for each man here, in the Philistine style—reds, blacks, or blues. If you cannot tell me the answer, you must give me thirty linen garments and thirty sets of clothes."

There was quick acceptance, and this was the high-water mark of their approval of me, because no Philistine can resist this sort of challenge. Maruck eyed Carillon thoughtfully, and then he answered for the lot of them: "Tell us your riddle. Let's hear it." And they all became stone silent.

As they settled in with their drinks, I answered, "Very well:

Out of the eater, something to eat;
out of the strong, something sweet."

Walking slowly amongst them, I repeated my riddle again, smiling. Some leaned back in their seats with their hands on their heads. Others flapped their lips. Most continued drinking. Maruck let out a large belch and wandered to the beer barrel for a refill. Staring hard into his mug, he said, "Samson, we will name your eater, and we will leave better-dressed men than we came."

At that moment, Dallim arrived with my parents and said I might go to my bride.

Chapter 17

Now, for the event that had consumed my thoughts and imagination since I first set eyes on Shealtah. I climbed the ladder up to the rooftop and entered the tent where she awaited. She smiled shyly. She was perfumed and dressed in red and white, a pure and perfect bride. She wore a silver poppy broach and an amulet of carnelian with a necklace of pale pearls. Her head was crowned with a wreath of flax in flower. On our bed were laid new sheets of Egypt—a wedding gift from Dallim, and what a luxury! Lavender and rose petals were spread over the quilt, and the bowl of mandrakes I had sent flying in Dallim's home an hour earlier had been carefully restored to an adjacent table—not that we had any need of such things.

I went to Shealtah and pulled back her veil. I kissed her, and...I came unto my own. When this was done, and done *properly* I will say, we dressed and presented the crimson cloth to Schmealnah, Aunt Hama, and some other ugly Philistine rag wench there for the occasion. They all nodded approvingly at the bloody stain, and hung it in the corner of the roof for the satisfaction of any busybodies who felt the need to confirm the terms of our marriage.

Shealtah said to her sister, "Now I have known a man, just like you."

"And a far better one at that," I said, squeezing her arm playfully.

But Schmealnah took great offense at this truthful comment, insinuating her sister did not respect her wayward ways—a claim for which she demanded an explanation!

The two began to argue vehemently about respect and relations and fatherly approval until I insisted that a woman's worth was never beheld in a sister's eyes, and they both had better hold their peace on the matter.

We climbed back down and out to the yard where the crowd waited, the women gave the signal to my father and Dallim, and the whole wedding party cheered and shook their tambourines and cymbals. My father put his arm around Dallim. Both men smiled and laughed and congratulated us with doting affection.

Rounds and rounds of toasts were offered in our honor—to me and Shealtah, to our health, our future, our children, our marriage bed; to Dallim and Schmealnah, her second helping and her donkey's poor back; to our families; to the mountains and sea, the sun and the moon. Whatever one man praised, the rest drank to with gusto. The barrels drained, the kraters emptied, and even my mother, who rarely partook in wine, allowed herself two cups of Dallim's finest red. Her tongue loosened and she began to advise Shealtah on how she might best "keep me in line." My mother spied me listening with amusement, and I laughed out loud at her embarrassment. She blushed and apologized, promising to keep her boundaries and let us cleave. But Shealtah put her at ease and thanked her, smiling sincerely and looking to me for affirmation. I kissed her fully again, and felt that shared union of love and joy, hope and inspiration in our hearts.

Late in the day, Dallim's servants carried in apples from his orchard. They also brought out dried figs, dates, and raisins from his storehouses, and shared honey cakes made especially for this occasion. Almond blooms and hyacinths filled the yard with sweet perfume, and the afternoon breezes brought forth the fragrance of late winter jasmine. Palms rustled, wind chimes rang, there was laughter and merrymaking...all was lovely, bright, and warm. It was the consummation not just of my marriage, but of my entrance to manhood and future possibilities. These are my memories from that day, a perfect day, when Israelites and Philistines fellowshipped together like people who are not locked in eternal strife.

I comprehended no darkness, yet shadows were fast approaching.

Chapter 18

That first night of the wedding feast, Uncle Morson and Aunt Hama prepared a delicious main course of beef steaks, plus barley and root vegetables. There was strong approval for the meal. Oil lamps burned joyfully well into the second watch, though Shealtah and I retired shortly after supper to enjoy the blessings of our new station.

In spite of the hubbub all around Dallim's home, I slept very deeply. And the next morning, Shealtah and I awoke quite late to the smell of catfish, which my mother and Aunt Hama fried on the hearth. Yet by the time we came down for our breakfast, Hama told me *my* wedding party had over-indulged; there were now just two filets left, and these of inferior quality. Shealtah sensed my irritation and held my arm tightly to her bosom, insisting to Hama and the others all was well; we would be more than content with grain and milk.

We sat with our meal across from Maruck and his followers, who lay recumbent against their cushions, well satisfied and full from the morning's feast. Each one had six or seven silver skins left on his plate! I was doubly annoyed that Carillon, our *trusted Philistine*, had also eaten heartily. He was clearly determined to become Maruck's footstool, applauding the man's wisdom, laughing at every joke, and endorsing all of his bravado.

"Samson, my son," Maruck said, rubbing his belly in decadent gratification, "you slept deeply, as a newly married man should. But you missed the catfish, alas."

"You missed it all right, Samson!" Carillon chimed in. "It was delicious."

"I tried to save you some," Hama said with annoyance. "That one—" she raised a scolding eyebrow to Maruck "—said catfish spoils quickly, and was best to eat right away."

"Yes, Samson, best to eat quickly," he echoed, wiping his sleeve across his greasy chin. "That is the rule with fish after all. Wake up earlier tomorrow, ha ha!"

Despite Shealtah's best efforts, my irritation remained. That afternoon, while she rested, I returned to the Philistines on Dallim's veranda with an eye toward making trouble. The venue at the rear of his home was shaded by a thick covering of grapevines. The leaves fluttered in the breeze, casting shadows that flickered and danced about, and many of the Philistines dozed. When Dallim came out and refilled the wine krater from his decanter, they all rose lazily to refresh their cups, too. Knowing they were sleepy and enfeebled by drink, I began to question them again about my riddle. "Perhaps Dallim has poured out the answer; perhaps it lies in the bottom of a barrel!"

Some grunted; others kept silent. They were annoyed as I hoped. Maruck said, "Samson, why don't you run along and pester your new bride and stop trying to ruin our wine." Turning to Dallim, he said, "Good master, this is excellent!"

Dallim bowed, but our conversation had captured his attention. He gave me a queer look and motioned me to him, whispering, "What's all this about?" Hearing my explanation, he frowned and left shaking his head.

After a time, I noticed a thread from a seam peeking out from under my arm. I said, "Look! This tunic will soon wear out. Where might I secure another? I know what I will do. I will have the Philistines deliver me a new wardrobe."

"That will be the day," they said. "We are close to solving your riddle." And they began to guess at answers until Maruck interrupted them.

"Samson, young lad, understand the lesson of the blustering fowler. He purchased a new snare on the promise of a basket of eggs." His eyes narrowed and closed as he continued, "Yet in the evening, the man returned from his hunt empty-handed. As a consequence, he lost his net and his shirt, and—" here his voice hardened and he stared at me "—he was beaten severely and thrown out."

Now, Pharaoh Ramesses had appeared toward the end of Maruck's story to beg for cake. Despite the priest's ominous fable, I was not finished toying with them. I said, "Here is an eater, hungry and true. Maybe he can help you!"

The Philistines considered the baboon a novelty for sport, teasing it with dates and other treats, but not a clue for the riddle. Nor did they know the creature's prior work experience, and I set to making that knowledge pay.

Fingering an empty date bowl, I said, "If only it were harvest! Pharaoh Ramesses might bring us all fresh dates to share. These animals are such excellent climbers, you know." I looked longingly up at one of the nearby palms towering over Dallim's home, though they were not in season.

This produced the intended guffaws and ridicule. They expressed disbelief any being with such paunch could scale a tree, but I had previously seen it climb around the roof and various low-hanging branches, mainly to taunt Dallim's dogs (though I kept all that to myself). Others compared it to Schmealnah, which I thought grossly unfair to the poor beast.

The Philistines asked me how I knew such a thing, and I said I heard it from the Ishmaelites, which was…indirectly true.

"The Ishmaelites?" they scoffed. "The Ishmaelites will tell a man anything to make a sale. *Anything*."

"No, it is true," I insisted. "If only there were ripe dates, you would see."

One of the men asked, "Would it also fan you with a palm and feed them to you?"

I smiled and said, "Perhaps, if I promised to return the favor."

Maruck said, "Samson, there are unripened dates atop the tree. Do you think the baboon would fetch some and vindicate the Ishmaelites' claims?"

And I said I supposed it might.

"Would you put 10 shekels on it?" Maruck asked, silencing the other guests.

This was the opportunity I was waiting for, and I feigned innocence. "I would put 100 shekels on it. But friend, do not lose your money. Pharaoh Ramesses takes no offense at your disbelief. Neither do I care if you believe or disbelieve the true words of the Ishmaelites."

"One hundred shekels it is!" Maruck cried. "Every man here is witness to our agreement. You have five minutes to train that fat-assed shoat."

Well, there was no small risk here, but I believed Pharaoh Ramesses had at least one more climb in him. Leading the baboon on gently to the tree, I pointed up to the fruits, grunting unintelligibly, which caused the Philistines much amusement.

But when their attention returned to their cups, I discreetly fed the animal a chunk of honey cake and showed it another piece as ransom for the dates—just like Dallim used to do. It was as I hoped—old habits kicked in, and the baboon immediately skittered up the tree, much to the amazement of the guests. When it quickly reached the halfway point, Maruck swore by Dagon that it was treachery.

"Only the treachery of a fool's wager," I was saying—but then Pharaoh Ramesses slowed considerably. Three-quarters of the way up, it paused, heaving so fiercely I half expected it to tumble down from exhaustion. When the baboon took a step back, the Philistines cheered and I began to worry how I might raise 100 shekels. But the break was temporary. Looking and seeing me wave the cake, the baboon rallied, rapidly propelling itself up the last section of the tree. When it reached the fronds, it grabbed the lowest and swung up to the top, snapped off a large cluster of yellow dates, and sat there regenerating.

Some of the Philistines began to argue that if Pharaoh Ramesses fell out of the tree and died, the bet would be nullified, since its return journey was not completed safely. But these faint hopes were soon quashed, because—after its momentary rest—the animal easily sidled back down the tree, all the while holding the yellow dates carefully in its free hand. These were handed to me in exchange for the other honey cake, which was swallowed whole. In spite of its triumph, the creature was clearly distressed, crawling over to its mattress, where it collapsed and continued panting convulsively.

Meanwhile, I walked over to Maruck, handed him the bunch, and said, "Here you have it—100 shekels worth of unripened dates, and I hope they please you well."

Feigning cheerfulness as he chewed one of the small, yellow dates with a bitter, puckered smile, Maruck demanded a collection from the Philistines to compensate for his own insufficiencies. He said the wager was made with encouragement; therefore, the debt belonged to one and all. He badgered them until he had raised 17 shekels, which he handed to me.

He said, "Take these as a sign of our generosity and good faith. This is all we have at the moment."

I scowled and said that in Israel, a man who bets more than he is worth very often learns he is worth less than he imagined.

Looking at the ground, Maruck said, "Samson, do not be consumed with greed." He paused, then looked up; there were daggers in his eyes. "In truth, you treat your guests too shabbily. Do not be like the greedy steward, who insisted on exact payment from a devil in disguise and received judgment for years of usury. Rather, accept that which is given to you, that it might go well with you and that you live to receive all you are owed."

Chapter 19

The next morning, Dallim was told how I collected 17 shekels from Maruck, and he panicked. He stormed up to the roof in a huff where Shealtah and I were still sleeping to demand I return the money and refrain from defrauding anyone else.

Seeing his sour face first thing upon waking put me in an equally foul temper, and I responded in kind: "Do not bother me about this, Father. I did not twist Maruck's arm. I begged him—*begged* him—to refrain from the wager, but he forced my hand. He called his companions as witnesses against me! And then he ordered them to settle his debt. He was hardly out three shekels, and I suspect he stole those from his temple."

No, I did not return the money then, and I did not feel any guilt over the matter. But Dallim was indignant; he threw up his arms and stomped back down the ladder, nearly killing himself when he slipped and fell through the last few rungs, cursing my stubbornness loudly as he crashed onto the floor.

"I suppose he will blame his bruises on me, too," I said bitterly. Shealtah stayed quiet.

After a dramatic display of moaning and rolling about, Dallim limped off to complain to my father, insisting he forbid me from "swindling" any other guests. My mother and father came to me in grave concern. When I told them the particulars, they asked if it was wise to deal thusly with such an influential Philistine. But if I began to doubt myself, I found Carillon and Schmealnah avoided me, and this I counted in my favor. Maruck himself gave me the evil eye, but that was entirely appropriate for such a depraved being.

Shealtah was much more fearful. She spoke barely a word through the morning, until we retired for a midday nap. As we lay there, she warned me, "Samson, Maruck's reputation is well known here. He is a man of violence who always does what ought never to be done." I knew for certain then I would not see that money—or if I did, it should be handed over with a knife in the back. Despite these worries, I comforted her and we were soon asleep.

That night, the third of our celebration, was the high point of feasting. Brightly burning lamps were scattered about the tables and strung from the veranda's pergola. The Philistines' mugs of beer were filled and refilled, and the wine kraters were not neglected by any but my mother and me. Much to my annoyance, Shealtah displayed a strong taste for wine as well. And the more she drank, the more she whispered into my ear about bad omens and unlucky signs. This badgering was never exhibited during our betrothal, and it was exceedingly tiresome. Nevertheless, for the sake of unity, I assured her repeatedly that we should be careful.

My parents provided delicious roast hens for the dinner, seasoned with salt and desert herbs, but they prepared them on the hearth in the Philistine style according to the tastes of our host.

We had barely begun eating when Maruck, seated at the far end of the long table, stood up to address the entire party. Complimenting Dallim's hospitality and my family's meal preparation, he complained bitterly about being tricked into a bet at a time when his wits were softened by wine, comparing it to stepping on the plow end of a hoe and being struck in the genitals by the handle. Of course, he and his companions were certain no harm was intended, and they were more than willing to forgive. That is why he had prepared a special ceremony for me and Shealtah—one never seen before in Philistia, but one all Philistines and Israelites of good faith would certainly agree was highly appropriate for such a joyful occasion.

Proceeding to unveil a wormwood cup wrapped in mugwort, he said, "This cup of holy water was boiled with bitter herbs and distilled before the great god Dagon with juices from the vines he favors. Samson, drink this now to honor Dagon. Drink it in fellowship, Samson, to your wife, your host, and your brother Philistines."

Under friendly circumstances, I never hesitated to discuss the Nazirite vow assigned me before birth. But at this moment, I felt such an excuse would only encourage further strain with that uncircumcised idol worshipper. And I saw the shock and anger on my parents' faces, too. So I answered plainly, "No."

"Do not be rash, young Samson. Think carefully. How will you live in peace and safety if you reject our sacrosanct rituals?"

"No," I said again, more firmly this time. I stared defiantly at him, and he back at me. The tension was severe, and Shealtah broke first, begging me to drink the ungodly concoction.

"Listen to her, Samson," Carillon squealed.

"No," I said to him. "No," to Shealtah. Pointing straight at Maruck, I stood up and said firmly: "No and no and no. You may as well ask me to drink Dagon's piss! The answer is no."

He squinted at me and rubbed his chin, smiling darkly. "Very well. I thought you might reject our fellowship offering. We are prepared to proceed another way—"

At that moment, there came a sudden clattering and rattling of metal all around. The incense candle holders were snuffed out and the lamps dimmed. The women screamed and Hama fainted, falling back over her cushion. The racket stopped as abruptly as it began, the lamps brightened with an eerie blue light, and Maruck cried out, "Behold the wisdom of a sage!" as he swept his scepter grandly across the table.

A voice arose like one calling from the bottom of a well, crying out haltingly, "At the destruction of the ancient kingdoms, when came the dawn of the Philistines, the great god Dagon left his ruined homeland and journeyed through the seas, carrying the Philistines in his mouth. He spat them out upon the shores of Egypt, but that land was a smelting furnace unfit for a sea people, and Pharaoh's hordes were well established in mighty stone fortresses. These proved too strong for those used to the cool, blue waters. Then the great god Dagon became angry with his people; he desired Egypt for them, and the call of Dagon is irresistible."

At this, the sharp rattling of metal resumed, the wind chimes crashed violently, and the lights dimmed again. After a brief flourish, the clatter stopped, the lights arose, and the voice continued: "Dagon forced the Philistines to construct reed boats, for he would not suffer them to return to his mouth when they tasted of defeat. He pulled them through the sea to Canaan. Upon the shore of their new home, and chastened by Dagon, our ancestors said, 'We have known the sea as our home; now let us take this land. We will fortify our towns and slay all who oppose us.' And Dagon answered them, gnashing his teeth and saying, 'Should any prove too strong for you, make sacrifice and call on my name, Dagon, for my call is irresistible and your enemies shall be washed away—in blood!'"

Just then, I sensed a presence on either side of me. There were two men with buckets of pig's blood or piss or some other foul-smelling swill, and they intended to douse me at the climax of Maruck's show. As they let fly, I sprang back.

One of their salvos hit Shealtah square in the chest, soaking her in filth as she gasped and sputtered. The other flew over the table and drenched Hama, shocking her awake from her faint.

Looking back, I will say this trick was original. I have never yet understood how the Philistines controlled the flames, nor turned them blue on cue, although I know they were banging forks and pans under the tables and in the shadows. All of that aside, when I saw my wife crying and soaked in that vile concoction, and heard Carillon pointing and laughing hysterically at Hama as she squawked and struggled to sit up and regain her senses, I was furious! I jumped up and ripped the bucket out of the hands of one of those sousers and slammed it down on his head. Turning to the other man, I grabbed him by the ear, pulled him to the edge of Dallim's yard, and kicked him into the brush.

There was great commotion, and Maruck demanded, "Samson, what have you done with those two men?"

I said, "I sent them to Dagon. They did not want to go, but there they are. His call is irresistible, you know."

Several of the Philistines were kneeling over the man I knocked out, attempting to revive him. One of these fellows was especially wobbly from drink; when he tried to rise, he lost his balance and staggered over his fallen countryman. Crashing into the table, he scattered plates, cutlery, and scraps across the veranda, fell back, and cracked his head on the ground. He lay sleeping alongside the other, both entirely unresponsive to all the "helping hands" around them.

In the torchlight, a big fellow named Ekmer—who had had his eye on me ever since I arrived with my parents—put his hands on my chest and threw me down to cheers from certain nearby Philistines. I gave him that one for free, but when he came to repeat the gesture, I hit him with my elbow across his chin and sent him crashing over the table. He landed atop the other two collapsed Philistines, the three of them all piled up like firewood.

Pandemonium and yelling ensued. Schmealnah was crying and laughing and making a scene. Maruck and his men cursed and yelled. But none of them stopped drinking. They continued filling their cups with wine and beer, even as they struggled to understand how their plans had failed. I watched them staggering around drunkenly until I was satisfied they intended no further harm that night. Grabbing Shealtah, I carried her off in the darkness to Dallim's well, where I stripped her down and washed off the foul stench of the Philistines. She protested the water was cold and began to cry, asking how I could treat her this way.

"You smell very bad," I said. "And you are drunk."

Suddenly her crying stopped, and she gripped my arm tightly. "Samson," she whispered, "I am naked. They are all going to see me naked."

I said, "Shealtah, I am bathing you, yet I cannot see you naked. You are safe in the darkness."

She began to panic and laugh in equal parts. "Do not let them see me! I will be a laughingstock. What would my father say?" I hushed her. She was quiet for a moment—until the washing tickled her. Then she erupted in uncontrollable giggles. When these ceased, fear returned to her voice: "I do not want that man Maruck to see me. He is repulsive. Did you hit him, too?"

Once she was finally clean, I put her over my shoulder and carried her to the home, sneaking in the rear door and up the ladder unnoticed. The entire way Shealtah had to fight to withhold outbursts of laughter, and I could feel her shaking and convulsing as she struggled to keep quiet. Safely back in our tent on the roof, she became hysterical until her face was covered in tears. She was nearly asleep, but I kept her awake a while longer, even as the tumult on the veranda below carried on.

Chapter 20

If the Philistines had not consumed an impossible quantity of wine and beer, I verily believe they would have tried to slit my throat that night—though if they were as incompetent with blades as they were with buckets, Shealtah would have borne the brunt of their revenge.

The next morning, Aunt Hama and Uncle Morson departed immediately. I am sure my parents would have preferred to join them, although they were still obligated to the wedding party. Dallim and my father scrambled ostrich eggs for breakfast, providing a rich assortment of dried fruit from their respective pantries—dates and figs, which I enjoyed, and raisins, which I avoided. Foam on a silver jar gave way that Dallim's she-goats had been milked, but not a drop was saved for me or Shealtah.

In spite of their indulgence, the Philistines before me were a sullen lot, struggling with varying degrees of injury and inebriation. The lout I struck with the bucket had a large purple egg atop his bald head, while the one I threw into the desert brush looked like an overripe mush melon for all his cuts. Ekmer bore a deep gash across his chin, which he massaged continually while staring at me darkly. Many others were shielding their eyes from the windows and moaning about their headaches. Maruck looked asleep, and he clutched tightly a small statuette of that foul fish Dagon.

As Shealtah reclined next to her father and Schmealnah, I said in booming voice, "Good morning, men! Schmealnah, you are looking bright like the full moon today!"

Some groaned, others moaned, and Maruck hung his head.

"What is this, a wedding party or a physician's ward?" I cried out, slapping the table loudly. "You know this is a time for merrymaking, but you all look badly beaten—beaten worse than these eggs."

"Samson, for the sake of all the gods, quiet your voice," Maruck groused, wincing in pain. "Don't you know we are all hung over?"

"I am a Nazarite and have made a vow to God to drink no wine," I answered loudly. "And from the looks of things, you all should do likewise."

"Dagon requires no such vows," Maruck said quietly.

"He does not?" I said in the same voice. "But what if he did?"

"He does not," Maruck repeated, barely whispering.

I changed my tone to one more serious: "What does Dagon say about paying wagers?"

Maruck cracked his eyes and answered grimly, "He says young men should practice manners when they visit a guest's house in a foreign land, and if you don't like that, we can invite the priest of the Nephilim to arbitrate."

Dallim, who had been listening nervously, cried out, "There is no need to bring them into this!"

Shealtah interjected, "Samson, be gentle with these men. They are my brothers."

"He is bluffing," I said. "The Nephilim worship Molech, not Dagon. Besides, Maruck knows he will not get another drop of wine if those giants show up. I have watched them drink. They are not likely to share. Then he would have to spend his own money on wine, and he would sober up in all likelihood, as he is not one to surrender a coin willingly."

"You damned rat pig Hebrew!" he growled, staring fiercely at me. "I already paid you more than I should have. What sort of man swindles his own wedding guests?"

He picked up his mug and gulped it down, which left a shiny white smear across his upper lip. Scowling, he threw the vessel against the wall, shattering it to shards. "You come to our land, take one of our choice women, reject my fellowship offering, and—" he looked at the three men who bore marks "—*brutalize* innocent people, and you have the nerve to demand money you did not earn? I will tell you about Dagon, then: he frowns over any unpaid debts, especially dishonor!"

With that, Maruck stood up and flipped his whole section of the table, dumping dishes, food, and cutlery across the floor. He yelled, "You will be paid in full, right now!" and spittle flew from his lips.

The women screamed and Dallim cried out, "No!" He came between us, pleading with Maruck not to fight. But the priest was a large man, and he easily threw him off. As he pulled out a long knife from his belt, I snapped off a broom handle to defend myself. But as fate had it, Maruck stepped on a portion of eggs he had knocked to the floor. His feet flew out from under him, and he landed with a hard "crack" on his back and head. Like that other fellow the night before, he lay there fast asleep—yet another self-inflicted wound for these Philistines.

More men came running to the room. When they saw their leader stricken and me standing there with a broken broomstick in hand, they demanded an accounting. My father, who had been standing next to me, told them that Maruck had slipped. He kneeled to attend to him, asking for water and a pillow.

Ekmer said he had just witnessed a miracle—eggs that saved a man's life. He made a move for me, intending to continue what he had begun last night. He said he was not drunk this morning, and I said I would gladly accept that excuse and beat him a second time. But Dallim was back on his feet, and he came running between us and grabbed Ekmer, yelling, "No, no, no!" He turned to me angrily. "Samson, you have carried strife into my kitchen."

"Me?" I cried. "Did I flip your table? Did I pull a dagger— or drink all the milk?"

My mother had been waiting on the Philistines, and she made a clumsy effort to tip over the wash bucket. "Oh, Samson, look what I have done," she interrupted, moving boldly between me and the Philistines. "Won't you fetch me more water to clean this mess?" She grabbed my arm forcefully and pulled me away quickly, whispering to come along so tempers might cool.

"These glutinous Philistines will leave us destitute," I said when we were a dozen feet from the veranda. "It will take years to pay off their drunkenness!"

"Samson, they are stronger than we are—here and in Israel. Therefore, we must not incite them, Samson, or else the men from Gath will return sooner than any of us hoped." She always used my name repeatedly when she was lecturing, and she continued: "Samson, go get the water. Take these buckets, Samson, and do not be in a hurry. I will attend Shealtah and smooth out the rough spots, and you must cancel Maruck's debt publicly. Let his bruises count for full payment. Do this for me, Samson. For me."

Everyone was against me, even my mother! I stormed off through Dallim's palm groves, past the wells, through the vineyards, to a slight hill where I sat underneath an oak looking towards our land, and beyond that the mountains of Judah. I remembered the Judahite champion Johannon, who had planned a stand against Philistine tyranny, only to be struck down by the Rephaite at Mahaneh Dan. What would he have done with a houseful of imbecilic mendicants headed by a degenerate like Maruck? Most likely, he would not have been here in the first place.

As my anger boiled, I took the broom handle, which I had gripped tightly since the "dustup" with Maruck, and beat a small grouping of mushrooms until they were nothing more than a smear on the hillside. If only they had been Philistines! Nevertheless, this outburst relieved me to a certain extent, and I made a slow return to Dallim's home.

Chapter 21

Scattered about Dallim's rooftop patio were a number of flowers, berries, and fruit trees growing in diverse painted pots. I had buried the 17 shekels Maruck gave me as "down payment" in one of these with a rock rose in early flush of blooms. Digging out the coins, I made my way down to the veranda, where that sham priest was recovering.

If given the chance, I knew he would pocket the entire amount without making any effort to reimburse those who had answered for his debt—and their anger would remain on me. So I deliberately made a show of handing Maruck the coin bag in front of the others, proclaiming to all that I trusted him to return the coins to their rightful owners (which was actually me, though I repeat myself). My hope was to expose the man for the scoundrel he was, to drive a wedge between him and the others. But this was a futile effort, because *every* Philistine leader is a scoundrel. In truth, the Philistine people recognize no other sort of authority, but rather aspire to villainy themselves.

Maruck was lying atop a hammock with a bandage on his head, surrounded by inebriated minions. Schmealnah was also there, feeding him grapes provocatively and fanning him with a small palm frond. I thought: *Here is a pair of swine that deserve each other!*

With money in hand, Maruck made a big show of telling me all was forgiven, as if I were somehow indebted to him. He said to the crowd, "Boys will be boys," and he was grateful the eggs kept him from inflicting a regrettable beating.

I was about to argue the point when I felt my mother's eyes boring into me fiercely. Instead, I merely answered, "Yes, that would have been regrettable for you."

However, I can say a certain measure of peace did return to the home—for a few days at least. During that time, I neither threatened nor felt threatened by any man, though the Philistines continued drinking to excess and guessing poorly at my riddle.

Now, I will tell you how the wedding celebrations came to an end, and with them my marriage.

My habit that week was to lay with Shealtah twice each day, before our afternoon nap and again before we went to sleep for the night. As a result of this continual intercourse, I slept very deeply, and I thought nothing of it if Shealtah was not by my side when I awakened. But on the fourth day of our wedding, after we lay together in our tent, she threw herself on me and sobbed, saying, "You hate me! You don't really love me. You have given my people a riddle, but you have not told me the answer."

I said, "How can you say that? Of course I love you. I married you! I chose you over any of my own people."

She said, "Well, since you have not told me the riddle, it does not *feel* like you love me."

"Well," I said, "maybe you will *feel* differently when you have calmed down and had a nap."

She turned away from me and wept quietly, but not so quietly that I could sleep. I sighed, hoping she would settle in, but she would not receive the message. At last I said, "Look, I have not explained the riddle to my father or mother, so why should I explain it to you?" And I said other comforting things to her, but she refused to be consoled. Rather, she grew angry, but at least she stopped weeping. Perhaps if I had somehow fished out of her the explanation of her sudden curiosity... but

I was very tired, my strength was spent, and the air was warm. Therefore, being unable to reason with her, I fell asleep.

That night she repeated the issue before we lay together, but I made it plain I had no interest in the discussion. Then she slept with me most reluctantly, so there was little enjoyment in it for me, and I went to sleep sulking. The next afternoon was the same, and I punished her that night by withholding my love from her. Though she cried whenever we were alone, begging me for the riddle's key, I refused to unlock it for her.

She remained frigid toward me, and the following days were generally unhappy, until the morning of the seventh when a change came over her. That morning as we climbed down the ladder and walked out to the veranda for breakfast, she pressed herself against me affectionately and said, "Oh, Samson, let us take our afternoon nap early."

As it had been two days since we slept together, I happily agreed. I might have taken her right back to the roof then, if we had not just come into plain view of all the guests, including my parents. In my impatience to lay with Shealtah, the morning hours passed slowly, and I found the Philistines even more boorish than usual. Finally, we retired to our tent and resumed intimacy.

As we lay drifting off, she confessed to me how desirous she was for the answer to my riddle, which she said was surely the best she had ever heard and was driving her mad with curiosity. "You know how women are," she said. "We cannot put these things out of our heads. We shall be thirty suits of clothing richer. Tell me, Samson—you have worn only two tunics this entire week, and they look nearly the same. What will you do with thirty?"

I had no use for such an extensive wardrobe and intended to sell most of them. "Besides," I said, "you Philistines mix your wool with Egyptian linen, but Israelites wear only one or the other in a given day."

I had nearly fallen asleep when she resumed speaking in a quiet, whispery voice: "These wedding crashers have been awful, Samson. I cannot stand Philistine men. Everything will be different when we return to your home. I will be your help-mate, and you will be my champion, my prince."

Kissing my princess and closing my eyes, I had dozed off when she interrupted my peace once more. "You know, I am quite certain I have solved your riddle."

This caught my attention, and I returned to a state of alertness. "Indeed," I said, looking at her with tired eyes—though I did not believe her.

"The answer is our wedding, here and now. The Philistines are the eater, because they have eaten their fill. They are strong in numbers and appetite. When you win the wager and sell the clothing, you will thus gain the money to feed your family. That will be the sweet part."

I relaxed, for she was as far away from the answer as the east is from the west. Closing my eyes again, I laughed quietly and smiled, which offended her, but by now I could no longer stay awake. Just as I began dozing, she disturbed me yet again. "This time, I think I know for certain. Tell me if I am correct. Is it—"

"Shealtah, will you speak through until supper?"

That was not well received either, and she took a harsh tone. "Don't I have a right to guess, the same as all the others? What is this grief you are giving me? I slept with you, didn't I? Does this pillow talk really overburden you?"

"Shealtah," I yawned, "I am tired and well satisfied with you. And if you will close your eyes, I will whisper in your ear." For sleep's sake, I explained the answer to her, put my arm tightly around her, and at long last fell into a deep slumber.

Chapter 22

When I awoke, Shealtah was still lying there in perfect peace. As I had so often before, I stared at my beautiful bride in quiet admiration. Surely, there never was a woman like her—perfect in form, enchanting in laugher, with a youthful smile that might've conquered the most stern-minded king. I pondered how my life had changed, and rapidly: In the spring, thoughts of marriage were as far from me as next year's harvest. But from the low of Mahaneh Dan to this present high, I had a wife who would be the envy of every man in Israel and Philistia. I would never tire of her, even when I was old and grey and surrounded by grandchildren.

Oh! If only I had learned sooner the Philistines had threatened her life with fire. If only I could have made an example *then* out of Maruck. How I curse myself for believing they would provide due recompense!

Driven by fear, she used her beauty to weaken me, and when I fell asleep, she revealed to them my secret.

What a fool I was! But then…women have always been my weakness. Every loss I ever suffered was under the delicate hand and gentle touch of a beautiful maiden.

To get right down to it, though: I stood, splashed water on my face, and waited for Shealtah to awake. It was the last night of wedding festivities, and I sang quietly in eager expectation of a marvelous victory that would humiliate the Philistines and compensate my family's heavy wedding expenses:

You who ride on white donkeys,
sitting on your saddle blankets,
and you who walk along the road,
consider the voice of the singers at the watering places.
They recite the victories of the LORD,
the victories of his villagers in Israel.

I was just about prepared to add a new verse that would be a lasting rebuke to these drunkards when I smelled beef on the fire, the final course provided by my parents. Shealtah, however, seemed determined to sleep through the new moon. When clearing my throat and a coughing fit failed to wake her, I rolled her over and kissed her. Her eyes fluttered and closed, and she smiled. Her hair covered one side of the pillow, and she smelled of aloe.

"Samson, my love," she said dreamily, "is it time to awake already?"

"I smell supper cooking. Let us go—I have longed for this feast!"

She yawned and rolled away from me, stretched and stood; washed her face, and put on her broach and necklace. She smiled nervously, which I attributed to uncertainly about leaving her father's home for the first time.

"If only we could run away and leave all this behind," she said. "I could have you all to myself."

"Enjoy this last night in your father's house. Tomorrow will come soon enough, and I have a collection to make first."

At the table, Maruck and his companions looked especially glum, which I took as a sign they had conceded defeat—though they ate heartily enough. The beefsteaks, a final gift from my parents, were apparently delicious. But I took no notice. My thoughts were on the riddle's wager.

Finally, the meal came to an end, and with it the day, for the sun was far off in the western sky. There was a chorus of loud belches around the table, and I stood and slammed my cup down. "Well, have you fellows got an answer for me or not?" I spoke confidently.

Maruck, that sly dog, looked at me queerly. "Samson, my son, your riddle is a strange one, like nothing I have ever heard—" and here, I thought he was going to ask for a reprieve of the debt. Instead, he paused and sighed, asking softly, "Will you please repeat it for us all?"

This I did, and waited. My heart was racing. Silence and tension filled the room. Maruck looked around the table at his men. His lip curled slightly, and he said, "Well, what do you all say? Do we have an answer for Samson?"

"Give it to him! Give it to him!" they shouted, cheering and banging their silverware and cups on the table.

The game was up. The Philistines had not been downcast at all, only playacting; the entire spectacle was planned, and I was the goat. My parents were oblivious, and Shealtah stared bitterly into her plate. She would not look at me or anyone else but her father. Carillon, who had spent all his time at Maruck's feet, could hardly contain his delight, and the others wore similar expressions of glee.

"Samson, Samson, Samson, my son," Maruck said. "What is sweeter than honey? What is stronger than a lion?"

I hardly heard the words come from his mouth. I was looking at Shealtah. She was crying, head in hands. "What have you done?" I hissed, but she made no reply.

"Do not blame the woman, Samson," Maruck chided to cheers and agreement from the others. "Your riddle was a good one, but I have heard better."

"If you had not plowed with my heifer, you would not have solved my riddle," I growled.

"What does the Lord *your* God say about paying debts?" he asked, raising his eyebrows and tilting his head.

His companions all chimed in: "Do not be a poor sport. Pay up!"

I was furious. I was enraged. Fire came over me. I said, "I will show you what the Lord my God says about debts. The Lord himself give me strength to repay you—to repay you in full!"

In the midst of their rowdy exultations and laughter, I heard Carillon's high, piping voice over the rest: "I want a white tunic and a new blue robe, one with the cuffs and sash."

If I had stayed, I would have killed him. I might have killed them all, just as they deserved. Instead, I ran to Dallim's stable, seized his donkey, and raced into the sunset.

Chapter 23

In burning anger I chased the sinking sun across the desert plain, to the west, to the land of the Philistines. For many hours I drove Dallim's spoiled, barn sour donkey mercilessly, whipping the beast until its disagreeable attitude broke and it accepted the journey at hand. As the sun disappeared beyond the horizon, the full moon arose behind me like a signal light from a faithful friend, revealing the path I should go. Toward the middle of the second watch, I reached the streams that water Lachish.

Through the night hours, I watched Orion follow the moon on an ordered course. Some stars fell away in streaks of light. But when these all were hidden at dawn, I took in a new smell I soon discovered was the great sea. Riding up a dune, I saw a powerful city upon the water's shore. It was safeguarded by a long, high wall that curved out from its northern end to its southern. Two hills within rose over the rim of the wall; the northern was dotted with stone homes that must have belonged to wealthy nobles, while the southern was crowned with a palace. Suburbs extended from outside the wall well into the plain. And I thought: *How did they build such walls?* Surely Israel has nothing to match, and that is why the Philistines rule over us.

Though all the armed men of Israel might be helpless to tear down such battlements, I planned to sneak in, seize the wardrobes of one or two absent Philistine lords, and hurry on my way before any authorities were wiser. At least, that is what I had in mind at first. It was an ill-conceived scheme made in haste and anger. But the truth is, I never came close to those luxurious mansions on the hillside or to anyone wealthy at all.

You see, in those days, the lowliest born Philistine remained content in his squalor so long as he could hold his nose up to a Hebrew. Philistia's leaders secured the rights of no foreigners save Egyptians or Assyrians, tacitly encouraging their people to heap insults and abuse on travelers who did not come in large caravans bearing wares for their markets.

And thus as I will show, I was incited to violence almost immediately, as soon as I reached the outermost villages. The land here was sparse and impoverished. In the early morning light, I saw three pig farmers culling their herd and loading the carcasses onto a cart. They did their slaughtering in plain view of the other pigs, causing the entire parcel severe distress, and the commotion in their pen was very loud.

Approaching them directly, I hailed the men and asked, "What city is that with such a high wall?"

I waited to the point of embarrassment for a response, but they refused to hear me over the grunting and squealing of their animals.

"What city is that?" I asked more loudly, moving closer—but still they ignored me. Instead, I heard them say to each other, "Who is this bold fellow?"

My anger burned against them as if they were Maruck himself, and I warned them to answer quickly.

When they did not, I dismounted from the donkey and walked up to them with chest out. One of the pig farmers had a half-decent tunic. He saw me peering at him and said, "You are a long way from the mountains, donkey driver. Can't you comprehend we are busy?"

Another said, "Here is a Hebrew who thinks we Philistines owe him an explanation."

The third, who was closer than the other two, leered at me. Wiping mud from his brow, he said, "It is Ashkelon, you damned fool. Were you born yesterday? Be off with you before we slaughter you for the pigs. We do not have time to answer your ignorant ques—"

There was an unused ploughshare sitting against their pen. Before this man completed his insults, I broke the handle off and battered him over the head. His skull broke in, and he died. In shock and disbelief, the other two came cursing and hollering at me with iron goads. The first swung clumsily and missed badly, tripping and crashing into his own cart. When he rose, I bashed his head so fiercely that he flipped over the side railing and into the cart bed, where he lay dead with the other swine. I seized his goad to fight the third man, who motioned as if he were going to attack. But when he saw his partners brained, he thought better of it, dropped his goad, and ran. I threw mine at him, and the heavy iron end caught him in his upper back. He fell gasping, and when I reached him, he could not even form the words to beg for his life. I crushed his head, too. Then I stripped their linens and tunics, scored the bodies, and dumped them into the muddiest end of the pigpen. And I heard squeals of delight as I led donkey and cart away.

Now, I will concede it was a sin for a Nazarite to undress these dead wretches, just as it was to take honey from the lion. Yet it was no worse than they deserved.

Afterwards, I killed two more men on a neighboring farm and another on an adjoining property. When I struck down the last, his wife emerged from the home and shrieked at me, so I slapped her and threw her back inside, barricading her door shut. I moved on to the other surrounding farms and homes, crushing skulls and breaking bones with the iron goads I acquired. Before the gates of Ashkelon were opened or any real hustle and bustle begun in its outer villages, I had twelve sets of clothing and a cart full of dead hogs to show for my labor.

As the morning sun rose higher, I approached the city. High above on the wall, the blowing of a trumpet signaled the changing of the guard. When that was completed, the gates were opened and a considerable rabble lined up outside, perhaps numbering in the thousands, began to file in. I headed that way myself, entering Ashkelon midmorning, posing as a slaughterer in search of a butcher. I led my donkey and wagon in concert with the stream of people down the main road, which was lined on either side by wall-to-wall buildings, booths, and fruit stands.

We carried on to the crowded marketplace where countless vendors were buying and selling, bartering and finagling. I had never seen anything like this. In Zorah, we had a man who delivered salted beef once in a blue moon. The babble rising from all these merchants, traders, shoppers, and slaves—coupled with occasional cries from soldiers demanding one group or another "make way for the Seranim" or "make way for the Seranim's guard," or his general or chief of staff or whatever rogue needed access—was staggering. I believe every other Ashkelonite had some sort of role or title from the Seranim, and these were valued chiefly to lord it over lower ranks on the roads.

Without knowing anything about the going rate of pigs, I resolved to avoid any haggling with these Philistine pikers, who love nothing more than to knuckle under whichever poor rubes wander into their stalls. If they are selling, they set their hearts on forcing the highest price on record; if buying, the lowest. They brag to the other vendors about whatever amount is secured, and this goes out like a signal call—a challenge each Philistine sets in his heart to beat. They spend every waking hour fixated on this knavery, training for bad faith negotiations like Grecian wrestlers.

Soon enough I found one of these scoundrels—a meat vendor with extraordinary diverse offerings, including dogs, chickens, fish, oxen, pigs, and more. He had more meat than my family and our servants could eat in a year, spread on tables or hanging on hooks in his stall. An assortment of leather skins was stacked high on a table, and the man's sons were filleting goats and rabbits, dividing the meat, applying salt, and so forth.

Once he had finished servicing his Philistine customers, I suggested to him a price for the pigs that surely would have infuriated their previous owners, if they had only been alive to disapprove. He looked at me suspiciously and asked about their freshness, and I invited him to examine the meat for himself, assuring him they were slaughtered earlier that morning. He gave them a cursory look, called me a money grabber, and counted out half the silver I demanded—which I readily accepted, having paid nothing for the pigs in the first place. He asked if the clothing came with the pigs, but I said the haberdasher was my next visit.

He said it ought to be the washer on account of the smell.

His sons unloaded the cart, and I led the donkey and wagon on foot away from the busiest section of the market, down a street running south toward the palace, until I came to a two-story inn in the heart of the city called the Egyptian House. I was tired and hungry and longed for a meal and a nap after my all-night ride. But when I entered, a surly, sour rascal behind the counter with a venomous scowl and squint-eye ordered me out.

I asked him, "Where can I go for a bed?"

He said he could not recall a single inn in all of Ashkelon that kenneled flea-ridden dogs, and I had better head back to whatever cave I crawled out from. Well, he was lucky there was a contingent of soldiers breaking bread in his foyer, otherwise I would have shown that wretch what happens when you rile and insult this "dog." As it was, I vowed to visit him later to repay these insults, and I will tell you soon enough how I fulfilled that pledge—although it was not without trouble.

Midday approached, and the streets were hot. Crowds thinned, vendors closed, and the general hubbub died down considerably. I was increasingly tired and my mind clouded. I searched at random, turning here and there, hoping for an inn, but at last I settled for a brothel.

Based on prior conversations with Carillon, I was confident this place would be less selective than the Egyptian House, so I tied the cart and donkey and walked up its steps. At the top, a fat, broad-shouldered pimp in a leather jerkin grunted at me: "Pick one four shekels, pick two seven." Like the meat vendor, he had his "products" on display—women to suit every taste, all peering out expectantly from the front windows. I answered that I wanted only a bed to sleep on, nothing more. Some of the girls were disappointed, and the pimp was surprised. "No girl?" He paused for a moment. "Seven shekels!"

I had plenty of silver in my pocket, and when I agreed, he led me through a dank hallway and down stone steps into a dirty, grimy stable that led out to a quiet alley in back. He showed me to a row of stalls with fresh hay, and I selected one in the corner. The pimp ordered a particular girl to bring my donkey and wagon from out front to the back where I could see them. She wore a red frock and appeared competent with livestock.

"You handle the donkey well enough," I said. "Are you a farmer's daughter?"

"Not so far as I know," she said. "The wealthy merchants all ride in on horses, donkeys, or camels, and it pays to know how to handle them—and the merchants."

"I am not a merchant," I said, tipping her a few coins to keep a watch on the donkey. She said that was unnecessary, as the smell was more than enough to keep away any thieves.

"Nevertheless, it has not kept away your customers," I said, handing her the coins.

She said, "I spoke of the clothes in your cart." But I was already falling asleep, and I shooed her away.

Chapter 24

My rest was tormented by foul dreams of a deceiving wife. But when I felt Shealtah pulling me to bed with her, I found myself being awakened by the same Philistine whore in red, intent on coming to bed with me! I jumped up in a huff and rejected her services, insisting she keep watch on my property as we agreed.

She pointed to the cart and donkey and said, "Look for yourself—all is well. Come now and lay with me—no charge." And she asked if I ever had the pleasure of a Philistine wench.

I said, "Yes, I have, and one Philistine wench is enough."

I had slept for nearly three hours, twice as long as I intended. Though strengthened, I worried I could be trapped in Ashkelon for the night—a grave danger should any report of my actions reach city authorities. Therefore, I tipped the whore a second time, insisting she continue keeping watch over my property, promising more silver when I returned shortly. But I did not lay with her.

Having concealed a goad against my left thigh, I departed the brothel in great haste for the Egyptian House. I intended to repay the squint-eye's insults, and to make his clothing pay for my wager.

Ashkelon was quieter than during the morning rush. Most merchants sat lazily in front of their stalls; some were already closing shop. The sun was well along in the western sky, and I reckoned there were little more than 90 minutes before the city gates shut. Indeed, Philistine traffic ran exclusively in that direction.

When I burst into the Egyptian House, that old squint-eye was serving drinks to a handful of drunkards. The soldiers were all gone. He raised his fist angrily and said, "What are you doing back here, buzzing around like a damn fly that will not leave? Go find a streaming pile of, of—*what are you doing?*"

Before he could finish his abuse, I surged across the room and seized that ugly wretch by the throat, slamming his head down on the counter. He squealed to his customers for assistance, but I warned them: "This lowlife villain is deserving of death for his crimes. Why receive the same punishment when drinks are on the house?"

Three of those scoundrels reached over the counter to help themselves, such are the effects of alcohol on men who lack character. One other came at me, but I pulled out the goad and struck him down first. And I gave the squint-eye the same treatment. Then I battered the other three, who were each oblivious to their doom up until the second it devoured them. I stripped the lot, threw their naked bodies in the back room, and hurriedly tied up their clothes around the goad. This brought me up to seventeen sets. I also took two fresh loaves for myself, because I was hungry, and I hid four full wineskins in the bundle in case I should need a bribe.

Just as I was walking out of the Egyptian House, the door swung in with such force that I was thrown back over a table. If the clothing had not borne the brunt of the impact, I might have been knocked senseless. As it was, one of the wineskins burst, staining the garments crimson. While I lay there wondering what had happened, what should I see but a massive Rephaite entering. His steps shook dust from the ceiling, and he hunched down to keep from smacking his head on the rafters. I measured barely past his waist, and his cruel eyes, black and deep-set in his enormous head, gleamed with fierce wickedness. Resting a huge spiked club against the wall, he searched the room disapprovingly. I thought, "Lord, give me presence!"

When our eyes met, I was about to ask him if he was one of the three at Mahaneh Dan, but before I could speak up, he said, "Who are you, the laundry tart?" Then he picked me up and threw me through the lattice window down onto the street like I weighed no more than an old ash basket. Most people out there hurried along their way when they heard the crash, but a few neighboring shopkeepers laughed and said the giant was driving vermin from the Egyptian House again. That was the first time I was ever thrown, and I thought: there will be a better time to gain revenge against Rapha. Yet my bundle of clothing was still inside. Therefore, I had no choice but to return.

When I entered, the giant was eyeing the back room. He turned and glanced at me suspiciously. Shards of pottery and puddles of blood were everywhere. Sneering unpleasantly, he dipped his hand in blood atop the counter, sniffed it a few times, and ran his fingers slowly down the wall in a serpentine fashion, leaving a pattern of crimson snakes. "I knew it smelled like death in here," he said. "Well, you have spared me the trouble of settling old squint myself. I always figured he would come to a bad end, what with that evil eye of his and all."

His scowl deepened, and he stared darkly at me: "Son of Abraham, if you enter this place again, you will end up missing more than your foreskin." Pointing with his thumb back over his shoulder to the men I had slain, he snarled, "I will make you the crown on that rubbish heap." Then he picked me up, carried me toward the window, and threw me out to the street a second time. As I stood dusting myself off and conceding any of hope of regaining the clothing, the whole bundle came flying out the window with such power that when it struck me in the chest, I was knocked down into the dirt a third time.

With that problem having resolved itself, I hurried back to the brothel where the same disinterested pimp repeated his earlier offer: "Pick one four shekels, pick two seven." I grabbed him and threw him down onto the street below, just as the Rephaite had done to me, and he lay there face down in the dust. The whores came screeching, but when I slapped the boss madam, the rest quieted down and behaved. Proceeding downstairs to the stable, I found the one dressed in red sleeping in my spot. A quick review showed my carriage and its contents were all intact, so I left her a short stack of coins as promised, hitched the cart to Dallim's donkey, and set a brisk pace for the city gate.

The sun was setting, and the signal horn gave warning that Ashkelon would soon close. Rapidly I pulled the donkey, but when I passed the Egyptian House, there was an angry circle of men on the street surrounding the Rephaite, some wielding knives, cursing him as a murderer. He towered over the lot of them, keeping the mob at bay with his fearsome club. To my surprise and relief, he damned them all to hell, crying out that they were damn right he killed those men inside. "I ought to kill the lot of you ungrateful sons of whores," he thundered. Drunken or not, Rapha had incriminated himself in the hearing of many witnesses. By the time he sobered up and accused a Hebrew, I figured to be in Timnah, if not Zorah.

One of the Philistines ventured too close to the giant and was sent flying. The man's shattered, bloody frame landed mere feet from me, and when the Rephaite looked to his victim, his eyes met mine. He bellowed, "That Hebrew may know a thing or two about all this. Ask him!"

The Philistines looked at me, and some recognized me as the very one who was *twice* thrown out the window by the giant. Consequently, they perceived his words not as an accusation against me, but another threat against them. To aid their impression, I screamed, "Save me!" and cowered behind the donkey's barrel. The animal panicked at the sight of the giant, and we ran on faster.

The feint worked. I heard one of the Philistines answer angrily, "Yes, we know him. He is the one you tossed out the window."

Another man cried out, "He's the one who got away from you," as he lunged at the Rephaite with a knife. Like the great Judahite Johannon in the desert, this Philistine made a brave effort, but the giant picked him up like a child's doll and heaved him into the mob, knocking down seven or eight others. Constables and soldiers were rushing to the scene, and the commotion was a perfect distraction for my getaway. I thanked the Lord my God for concealing the truth from them, kept my head down, and rolled past the marketplace, past all the empty stalls and shuttered shops, and back up the main road to the city gates.

There, a company of soldiers had just begun closing the first of the massive doors—it took a team of four oxen on the outside and five men on the inside to push it on its heavy rollers—and as I drew near, an officer stopped me and said I would need to wait until morning to leave.

"Why?" I answered. "The other side is not closed. I can just walk out."

He said, "No! Once the gate begins to close, the way is as good as shut. Make arrangements, because you cannot leave until tomorrow morning."

"Why cannot I just walk out? There is plenty of room."

"It is the law of the Seranim, and the law is unbreakable. When the gate begins to close, the way is as good as shut."

"That is a stupid law," I argued, "when I could clearly just walk out and do no harm."

"Regardless, it is the law, and the law is unbreakable. And if I get any more lip from you, you can take it up with the jailer or else get striped here and now."

I remembered the three remaining flasks of wine I had taken from the Egyptian House and changed tactics. "Hey, brother," I said, "tell me, do you enjoy wine?"

His demeanor changed just as quickly. He smiled and said, "I would not be a good Philistine if I did not, no?"

Thank God Philistines love a good bribe. For the promise of drink, the man agreed to at least bend the Seranim's unbreakable law. I handed him the wine, and he called to the others: "Quickly, let this one pass! We do not want any Hebrews in here tonight, defiling our fair city."

So they let me exit Ashkelon, and the great gates creaked and groaned shut behind me, closing with a deep thud. From the outside, I heard the heavy chains and thick beams and locks and latches all being secured. When they finished, the horn sounded again, ending the city's business for the day. Forty or fifty yards out, I looked back; just as in the morning, the guards were changing high upon the wall, but now they were silhouetted against the sunset.

It should be enough to say that I secured the remaining thirteen suits of clothing on the outskirts of Ashkelon in the same fashion as I had that morning. I came upon Philistine townspeople in anger, and the best of them succumbed to my wrath. I doled out punishment in generous portion, just as they had done to my people for forty years.

Really, only one of these stories stands out from the others you have heard already, and I will tell it now.

When the stars had just begun to show and payment for my debt was nearly collected, I came across a lonely tumbledown home where the dull blue light favored by Philistine diviners flickered through the lattice window—the same sort of flame Maruck used for all his trickery at the wedding supper. I crept outside the door, listening for any men inside. After a moment, I discerned two male voices and one female, and I heard her gasp. She said, "These signs foretell of sudden disaster!"

With that, I knew God had put them all into my hands. I kicked open the door, flipped over the table that held their incense burners, and cried out, "Disaster is upon you!" as I clubbed the men who sought omens among colored stones. The fortune teller was an old hag, and I left her alone to exult in the fulfillment of her portent.

Her witchcraft was futility, was it not? If there were any real value to soothsaying, surely the stones would have aligned to warn these men of their fate instead of sealing it. But they saw it not. They were enticed to their doom by a lust for premonitions, and further, with these last pairs, I had the thirty sets of clothing Shealtah caused me to owe. While I had raced to Ashkelon in a fiery rage, I returned to Dallim's by the same desert path I had come the night before, stewing in anger under the moonlight at a far slower pace, because I was not eager to humble myself before the wedding crashers.

Chapter 25

For a time, Dallim's donkey pulled the small cart willingly enough; that old ass knew her way home. But her mood mirrored my own, and her enthusiasm slowly decreased until the third watch, when she required a half-hour's rest. We tarried on slowly afterwards, I alongside her, to delay the inescapable meeting with Maruck, Carillon, and the other Philistines—those moochers, leeches, connivers! The largest band of deceivers since the Gibeonite delegation.

My frustration grew with each passing step. At dawn's first light, with Timnah on the horizon, I took a pruning hook off the cart and began to beat every shrub along the path, cursing and battering them as if they were my enemies—until the tool gave way. I took up a rock and threw it at a hare. I smashed my goad on a boundary stone. I pulled up a young almond tree and swung it into a vineyard, cracking a trellis apart. If anyone had seen my fit on that road, he would have thought I was possessed of a demon.

But when the sun rose higher and its hot rays overcame the cart, the stench of the clothing grew so overpowering that I was forced to hurry along to keep ahead of it. If I had been more thoughtful, I might not have seized the tunics from pig farmers first. That was an error on my part. Had I delivered such foul garments to Pharaoh's grand courtyard, the insult may have sparked an invasion. But I doubted any of the wedding party would be particularly bothered, because every gathering of Philistines stinks to highest heaven anyway.

When at last Dallim's home emerged among the vineyards and date palms, it was late morning. I gritted my teeth and girded myself to face the dirty scoundrels who had come between me and my wife—who had ruined everything. Many were outside eating yet another breakfast "on the house." When they saw me, they made such a commotion that the rest were soon assembled, too. I spied Shealtah in the back of the crowd hiding under her father's wing, but I refused to look her way again.

Of course, that self-important, pompous buzzard Maruck made his way to the front of the lot. He took an oversized bite off a barley roll and chewed for some time before he began speaking, holding the rest of the Philistines in suspense. "Thampthun!" he said, swallowing the bite. "You returned. I never doubted you were a man of your word." He burped and spoke to the others, "Did I not I tell you he would pay his debts fairly?" As they gathered round, he eyed the clothing greedily, barely wincing from the smell, and rubbed his greasy fingers over the merchandise.

"Will you not wait half a moment?" I asked angrily, slamming my fist down on the cart's rail. I had journeyed two nights across the desert, risked life and limb, been insulted and threatened; I had tussled with one of the Rephaim and resisted a Philistine whore—all to pay off a debt I should never have shouldered. Delaying their satisfaction was the only arrow left in my quiver. "You come out like vultures greedy for the lion's kill, offering no water for my cup, no taste of bread."

"Ah, yes, excuse me," Maruck conceded. "Carillon, go and get your friend water to quench his thirst and a sponge for his feet. Oh yes, and a crust from last night." Maruck gave those orders, but remained close to the clothing. He had his eye on a particular striped tunic I took from one of the drunkards at the Egyptian House.

Moving closer, I asked him quietly, "Do you like that one, Maruck? The man who conceded it did not wish to do so. I fear it may bring you similar misfortune."

He let go the clothing, stuffed in the last bite of barley loaf, and answered condescendingly, "Eh, I thank huh mithforthune belongth to you, Thampthun. Yur wiff holdth too mush of an attathment to her peethul." He choked and doubled over, coughing and hacking. I made to leave, but he motioned me to wait while he hit himself in the chest a few times to force the bread down. Once he regained his composure, he said, "Personally, Samson, I eagerly anticipate your departure. I do not mind telling you I do not like you, although I wish you no particular ill will. Hebrews should stay among their own kind. But when you do return to your hills, Samson, I fear Shealtah's heart will remain here."

I said, "Indeed it will."

The Philistines stared impatiently while I leisurely washed my feet and ate the sour crust from Carillon. When my face puckered, Maruck said my parents left yesterday, and alas, the food Dallim had to offer was no longer quite so fresh or abundant. Still, I ate every bite, chewing slowly and deliberately, staring hard at those scoundrels until there was grumbling and Maruck told me to hurry up. "We cannot stand out in the sun all day, Samson. Gulp that down now, will you?"

When I finally finished, I told them, "Look and see! Here are thirty suits of clothing true to the 'Philistine style.' Wash them and be satisfied. My obligation is fulfilled."

Ruin my riddle, will you, Philistines? Cheat me out of my spoils? I think not! I fed you from your own plate when I made your kind answer for our wager. From your own neighbors I brought forth your plunder.

While those swindlers tore into the accursed clothing like jackals—may the accursedness transfer on to them—I entered

Dallim's house and bundled my spare tunic around my sole remaining iron-tipped goad. I was tying it all together when I felt a presence behind me. Shealtah was there in her traveling clothing.

"What is this?" I asked. "What are you doing?"

She was confused. "What do you mean? It is time for us to leave, darling," she answered. "Time to begin our journey together."

I answered coldly, "No, darling."

"No? Are we staying here?"

"You stay here, with your father and your people—where your heart is. I will return to mine."

The smile left her face. Anxiety showed in her eyes. "What do you mean, stay here? I am your wife!" she cried angrily. "You are taking me with you!"

"No!" I yelled, then quieter, "No" again. "Every chance you had, you took their side. In the evening, in the morning. In the beginning and at the end. You love *them*. You ought to have married that fat priest Maruck! Or one of his stooges."

Her eyes welled with tears, and she answered earnestly, "But he favors Schmealnah!"

"Ha!" I roared with false laughter, perplexing Shealtah further. She asked what was funny, but I only shook my head and said there was enough of her sister to please many men, and I should have anticipated the match.

"How can you leave me?" she sobbed. "I am tied to you. I have given myself to *you*. I do not want to marry a Philistine! I have given everything to you!"

"Not everything," I said. There was deathly silence while I finished preparing for the trip home.

Once I had done so and turned to walk out, Shealtah stole up behind me and wrapped her arms around my chest.

Her hot tears rolled down the back of my neck, and she said, "Samson, please—we just need to get away together."

But I did not return her embrace, and her weakness only served to harden my heart further. "I am sorry. We just need to get away," she sobbed. "I can make you happy when we are away. Then you will see. You will see why—"

"Then I will see why what?" I said, raising my eyebrows suspiciously at her.

She did not answer. She only cried, and continued waiting for me to return her embrace. But I never did. I did not know then, as I do now, that she acted as she did out of fear for her life. So I showed her no compassion. Her whimpering repulsed me. "It is as I thought," I said coldly. "Let me go. I have been here too long…too long." I pulled her arms apart from my waist, took up my things, and walked out.

Shealtah followed like a beaten dog, but I refused to look at her. She was too beautiful. She might have broken my heart if I had gazed into her eyes and acknowledged my responsibility for her crushed spirit. When I passed through the veranda, Carillon was sitting there on a bench sulking, his face downcast and distant. Sure enough, Maruck sat at a table next to Schmealnah, seducing her with a bowl of oats and a pan of cake.

I laughed cruelly. "Well, Carillon, one man plows, and another comes and seizes his harvest," I said. Schmealnah and Maruck looked at me questioningly, but if Maruck could not discern the bitterness written across Carillon's disagreeable face, I had no intention of enlightening him.

Just as I stepped down to the outer courtyard, Shealtah grabbed my arm again, sobbing even more hysterically. She made such a commotion that Dallim soon arrived with a handful of other Philistines.

"What is wrong with my daughter?" he demanded.

"Samson is leaving!" she blurted out.

It took a moment for him to comprehend the situation, but when he did, he said, "How can you do this? What about our agreements."

I replied, "I am going home, Dallim. That is all."

"Why?"

"He will not say, Father. He will not talk to me at all!" Shealtah cried.

"Why can you not explain this matter, Samson?"

"Because she is hysterical, Dallim. You know as well as I there is no reasoning with hysterical women. Now, goodbye!" I did not want to inventory my disappointments in his daughter in front of them all, especially when they were the cause of our undoing. In truth, I had little against the old man either; he also had been put out and abused by the Philistines, and his greatest misfortune was to be born one of them.

As I walked away, I could hear Shealtah wailing, and my heart was drawn to her. What would it be like going to sleep alone tonight? I nearly gave in. How I wish I had! If only I had. But my anger was too hot. And I vowed I would never humble myself before the Philistines again—not after that morning. Not after losing a wager I should have fairly won. Yet I dared not look back. I kept walking away—away from happiness, from the sanctity of a loving wife and happy home, and from the peace a man finds in his family.

Suddenly, I felt a hand on my arm. I turned. It was Carillon, asking if he might have a few days more before returning to work for my father. Shealtah's wailing had hidden his approach. I let fly a backhand that laid him out, turned, and walked away. I did not speak or look back again. That was that.

As I said, I did not learn then that Shealtah was threatened by the Philistines. Nor did I comprehend how my beautiful bride would ignite the conflict that followed. I only prayed to God that I would never see any of them again, but this too was futile.

Over the years, I have questioned many times how that day might have been different. And I have often wondered about the high price I paid for pride, though I believe it weighed out at a bargain compared to dishonor. That would have been too heavy a load to bear. But all of that is meaningless.

Now I have but one question: How can you Philistines justify your atrocious wedding customs? How can you burden young couples with dreadful debt, just so you ravenous hypocrites can enjoy a week of wine and feasting? You foist men like Maruck on unsuspecting families—scoundrels who would just as soon ravage the bride if the groom were not watching. And these are your people! What I mean to say is, go to hell with your accursed customs!

Chapter 26

When I was still a fair way off, I saw my mother at the height of our property, working around the pomegranates with some of her maidservants. As I drew nearer, my father also came into view by the almonds farther down the slope. Even from that distance, it was clear they had returned to their labor with gusto. There is such sweet fulfillment in the land, where God rewards the sweat and scrapes of summer with rich bounty at harvest. And I thought: if I pour myself into this work, I too will forget all that is behind me and find contentment, just as they have. But I dreaded our first meeting.

Once I arrived, my mother was the first to see me, and she inquired after Shealtah. I told her gruffly, "She is not here, and she is not coming."

My mother cried out, "What?" and when I repeated myself, she went running to find my father. They confronted me together, asking, "What is this all about?"

Bitterly, I conceded they were right: I should never have married a Philistine.

My father said, "How can you say that now? Do you know the expense we bore for your wedding?"

"I am sorry," I answered. "I will work without pay until you judge the debt fairly compensated."

My mother said, "One week ago, you insisted you loved Shealtah. How can you put her away so quickly?"

I told her, "I did not divorce her. I left her with her people, where her heart is."

"Did she tell you that?"

"Not in those words."

"Was she unfaithful?"

"What? No! I would have killed any man—"

"Where do you stand with her?" they demanded. "And where do we stand with Dallim?"

This got to the root of it, I thought. I assumed the nature of their dissatisfaction was chiefly financial, since they had opposed the wedding from the start, although I later learned this was incorrect.

To ease their concerns, I again promised to work diligently until they judged the money scales balanced. I also insisted they owed no further fruitage to Dallim—but they feared he would rally the Philistines against them to demand tribute.

"Shealtah is with her father," I said. "What do we have of Dallim's that we should owe a debt or face down a mob?"

"Nothing more than we had last time the Philistines came around," my father said.

I said, "You feared them when I was taking away one of their young women. Now you fear them because I am *not* taking away one of their young women."

But my father shook his head, and said, "Son, you will bring trouble upon us. This was a reckless decision, unwise and impulsive." He sighed heavily, looking down at the ground before he finished. "And you, Samson—you are the one who will bear the heaviest load."

My mother was crying. I raised my hands in exasperation and said angrily, "Then I will bear it if I can. Trouble will come whether or not I take a Philistine wench." I stormed off, but I concede now that my father's words were true, as my present station confirms. Alas, I was a young man and had too little patience for correction. I left Shealtah in a fit of stubborn rage, without any deliberation or foresight. Losing her condemned me to a life of strife and wandering, though it brought peace to many others.

Before I was out of his sight, my father called out, "Samson, one other thing: When the Philistines answered your riddle, where did you ride? Did you fulfill your debt, or should we expect them here to collect?"

I answered my debt was "paid in full." He wanted to know how I had wrangled up thirty outfits. To ensure they were never forced to testify under torture, I told them I traveled to Shechem, where I ran across a large caravan of Ishmaelites, hundreds strong. Walking up and down their line, I traded this and that, one thing and another, eventually negotiating my way from one tunic to thirty. My father looked at me suspiciously, but my mother was too distraught over my marriage to bother herself with any of this.

Yet this story caused me a new measure of trouble, as I will tell you shortly.

In the meantime, my parents were deeply dissatisfied, and they spoke quietly between themselves at great length.

I left them to their discussion; there was nothing else to do except pour myself into the work at hand—planting, pruning, fertilizing, picking. I resumed my chores alongside my brothers and the servants as if my wedding had never taken place.

At first, they congratulated me on my marriage, or inquired of Shealtah, or wondered when they might call upon me and my bride. I never made any answer, but only scowled, shook my head, or walked away. I spoke no words at all until they believed I had taken a vow of silence, and they left me alone. I kept to myself and worked, worked, worked, and became desolate and haggard.

Of course, word of my separation spread quickly enough around the property anyway, like wildfire, because no good story can be restrained.

Chapter 27

Discussions about Shealtah dried up like a desert stream, but my mind was consumed with thoughts of her. That frustration, coupled with a growing fear that my deeds in Ashkelon would become known, wore away at me. I began to see Philistines behind every tree and down every path. I felt hunted and alone and became abrupt in conversation. My parents did not understand what had come over me; gradually, the initial shock of my return wore off, and they were privately relieved I left the Philistine woman. They certainly did not miss being indebted to Dallim.

In the meantime, there was no shortage of work to be done. The abundance of the previous harvest, which was by no means limited to our property, forced my father to sell more product than he would have preferred on credit, across an area far beyond our normal business footprint. And this was in spite of the Philistines' ransacking of our stores.

Because of my increasingly impatient behavior, my father assigned collections to me, correctly assuming that time away would do me good. This was shortly after the Passover, before the return of summer, and I traveled with donkey and cart down to Sharon, or into the hill countries of northern Judah and southern Ephraim, usually to collect bushels of this or bags of that, or an animal or two. Cash payments were exceedingly rare, especially if the customers lived in a city. My father genuinely preferred bartering with rascal farmers like Dallim over indebting urban dwellers, who are less honest and more likely to renege.

While I was on the road, my spirit was untroubled by thoughts of Shealtah or the paranoia of vengeful Philistines. The miles wandering over plain or valley were a great catharsis. And by the grace of our God, I was untroubled by robbers or foreigners. These travels gave me cause to see more of the pleasant land, and they awoke in my heart a desire to visit new, far away places to escape it all, though this became yet another cause of grief in years to come.

My father very deliberately sent me only to those people he believed were honorable, and indeed they were—my presence was received with goodwill by my brothers and sisters, and their debts paid fairly and promptly. This included the vast majority of his associates, because most Israelites were not scoundrels like Maruck who dispute agreements or manipulate allies to a state of bickering. But there were a few unsavory ones—especially certain Benjamites.

Such was the case with a particular rival of my father's, one Zilphah of Gibeah, a merchant trader who was reluctant to fulfill his obligation, though he had indeed received his full measure of produce. City elders knew the man was a rascal, but they refused to condemn his thievery. Gibeahites are loathe to rule against their brothers, even when guilt is beyond question.

Now, regarding the clothing I seized from the Philistines in Ashkelon to fulfill the wedding wager—I had lied to my parents about that, to protect them in case my deeds became known. Due to the story I told about bartering with Ishmaelites, who as we all know are renowned for their haggling, my father believed I might negotiate an acceptable payment with that lawless dealbreaker Zilphah, and thus avoid a total loss for our family.

When he explained the situation to me, I resisted the assignment on principle. Once price has been agreed and product accepted, is not the time for negotiation past? "We ought to go and demand full payment," I said. "The compact is written in fired clay with Zilphah's own seal! The elders can see it for themselves." They had probably all been swindled by the man at one time or another.

Despite my reasonable objections, my father said that we would be fortunate to secure any payment at all, and based on my reputed success with the desert caravaneers, he insisted we would not reject an acceptable offer. He lectured that a little more compromise and a little less principle would still bring some reward, and when it came to debt, it was "better to be pragmatic and well fed than scrupled and hungry."

I bit my tongue, and we were soon on the road to Gibeah to visit that notorious piker.

Along the way, my father recalled how he had never had an easy time with Zilphah, and he was very relieved to have me with him. One year, the scoundrel had welcomed my father with a meal, but watched him closely and reduced his bill with every bite, right down to the last crust. Another time, he claimed an entire homer of pistachios was soured, though empty shells were scattered all over his front porch. He had also applied late fees, unloading charges, and every other post-exchange defrauding imaginable. My father warned me Zilphah would begin discussions by refusing to concede any debt, and we would need to "work him up."

His agitation grew as we approached the man's large home. It was in the center of town, with a stone foundation and a second story of bricks. As we walked up to his front door, I snapped at him, "Why do you trade with this charlatan?"

He whispered it had been years since they did business, and only the necessity of unloading product combined with a chance encounter brought them back together. His eyes narrowed as he banged on the door and called out, "Hey,

Zilphah, you old skinflint, we are here to collect. I brought my son. He's very good at negotiating!" This was a side of him I had never seen. I felt like a child being presented to the Levites for testing. He nudged me and said if I could turn one tunic into thirty, I ought to be able to get ten or fifteen shekels out of this fellow.

A shutter cracked from an upstairs window, and Zilphah cried out, "I have been expecting you, Manoah! I am sending out my own negotiator. He is very experienced. He will know how to—" he cleared his throat here "—*strike* a deal with you and your son."

The door opened, and an enormous bald man in a studded leather shirt emerged. As he chewed the last morsels off a chicken bone, Zilphah called down again, insisting we had come up short on some previous trade, and as far as he was concerned, the debt was squared. In fear, my father whispered to me, "Just tell him three or four." But before I could demand payment, the large fellow let out an enormous, stinking belch in our faces and flicked the chicken bone at my father, leaving a shiny grease mark across his forehead.

"What the hell do you want?" he demanded. And he made a fist.

"Look," I said, "pay us what you owe us—" and I slapped him across the face, knocking him down. He stood with a profusion of threats, but I slapped him down again, and I followed up with a kick square to the testicles that left him rolling about in agony.

When Zilphah understood his negotiator had been out-negotiated, he not only paid the thirty-five shekels owed, but agreed to a "late fee" of five more that I suggested, which I thought plenty fair considering his foul intentions. However, my father refused that money and gave back five more to care for the big fellow who lay there moaning throughout the conversation. I later heard from the man himself that he spent three days in bed before he could walk again.

On the way home, my father said he was surprised I fought so quickly. "Is that how you dealt with the Ishmaelites?"

"What could I do against an entire desert caravan?" I asked.

He said, "Samson, I think you would fight thousands if one gave you cause for anger."

I pointed out the large fellow actually struck first when he flung the chicken bone. And I said, "If I had followed your instruction, we would have more bruises but fewer shekels. Next time I should just stay home."

"Your mother will be happy with the money, at least," he said, "though it might be best if we did not share the particulars of your *negotiating*."

Chapter 28

When our collections were finally complete, I busied myself with chores and preparations for the fast approaching grain harvest. Never did I go anywhere without a knife or a billhook or some other weapon, although my fear of reprisals for my deeds in Ashkelon lessened with each passing day.

Still, in keeping busy from sunup until sundown, I sought from the work what it could never give—*peace*. Like tares in wheat, discontentment and unrest grew inevitably in my soul; I found no enjoyment in routine. As the days lengthened, my thoughts were increasingly consumed by Shealtah, and my bitterness intensified. Why had she taken their side? Why did she ruin our first year? It had been a full month since I walked away from her, and my anger had given way to questions—and desire. We could have been happy, just as she had said that last day…

For that matter, why had she said that? What did she mean? These questions perplexed me, whether waking or sleeping, and it told in my eyes. My mother grew concerned. She asked, "Why is your face always downcast? If you do what is right, won't you find peace?"

I grimaced and said, "That is what the Levites say, but I am not so sure anymore."

She sighed and looked far away, suggesting I might be suffering from the early symptoms of a certain illness, though assuredly not leprosy.

"Why would you say that?" I demanded.

"You look very pale," she said. "A mother notices these things. But we can rule out leprosy."

I just shook my head, but sure enough, I soon became ill, suffering in bed for several days—though not from leprosy. Nor was illness the root of my gloomy appearance.

The morning my fever finally broke, I took to roaming the hills above Zorah to regain my strength and settle my thoughts. Without considering any set path, I wandered far from home, going up one incline and down another, through a small canyon and out the other side. Passing under a particular set of cliffs, I scampered up their backside, step, notch, and boulder, until I reached an overhang overlooking the entire Valley of Elah. There I heard a certain moaning up a ways further, and I determined to investigate.

Quietly and carefully, I snuck up behind a mountain oleander and peered through the branches. Less than a stone's throw away, I spied a pretty young handmaiden of Israel—though one looking like Jephthah's daughter, with puffy eyes and tear-streaked cheeks. She stood among the reeds of a gentle mountain brook, picking iris flowers and releasing them in the water, where they rambled along slowly until they reached the cliff's edge and tumbled away down the side.

After watching her for a time, I stepped out and said, "Sister, why are you crying? And what is this unusual custom with the irises?"

She started, but eased when she saw I intended no harm. Looking back to the stream, she bent down to release another of the white flowers, watching sadly as it bobbed away. Her voice quavered: "The irises are in memory of my brothers, murdered by the Philistines. One is for the son of my mother; another I was pledged to marry." She paused and began sobbing again. "What is left for me but to join the other daughters of

Israel who are widowed before their time—before they bear children?"

The last iris passed into the current and out of sight as we stared into the water and listened to its gentle stirring. I admired her, even if her claims to full widowhood were dubious. I thought, here is a faithful sister, true until the end. And I naïvely began to believe Shealtah must be waiting for me in Timnah with a similarly contrite heart.

Finally, she said, "Look! You can see the hills of the Judahites from here. That is where I am from and where I will return when my days of mourning end. To the west, beyond the hills and on the plain, lies the land of our enemies, the Philistines."

Hoping to offer some small measure of consolation, I told her, "I slew thirty of the enemy in Ashkelon." She was the first I told.

"Then you are indeed a great champion, like no one else alive. Like one from days of old," she wailed. "Oh, that God would deliver us again." And she shed many more tears.

At last she steadied herself and returned to cutting irises from among the reeds at the base of the stems. But these she kept, weaving their ends into a wreath with the flowers on top. The crown reminded me of the one Shealtah wore at our wedding, and that sweet impression, coupled with this young woman's lovely virgin form, intensified my longing for my wife.

I looked to the west. It was a clear, cool day, and I thought: Somewhere upon that horizon, she is waiting.

The girl considered my solemn mood and asked, "Have you married your beloved?"

I had, I told her. She stepped toward the stream, reaching across to hand me the wreath she had tied. It glistened with her tears. "Here, take this to her," she said. "For the one I love is no more."

Wanting to honor the maiden, I said, "Very well, I will do as you say." We stood in silence for another moment until I began my journey home, considering all the while whether I ought to really return to Shealtah. That morning, my spirit softened considerably toward her, especially after my time with Rachel's bereaved daughter. I thought, "Maybe there is some explanation for why Shealtah betrayed me. Maybe she could provide an answer and we could still be happy."

By the time I recognized those familiar pomegranate trees atop my family's property, I concluded Shealtah was sufficiently chastened. And lo, I desired my wife! Immediately I would return to Dallim's to reclaim her. I mounted a donkey and lassoed one of our wandering goats to bring along as a peace offering. Before I left, my mother stopped me.

"Where are you going on that donkey with that goat?" she asked.

I told her, "To mend a broken tie."

She said, "Well, at any rate, it is good to see you looking restored."

Chapter 29

There was no unusual adventure on the road to Dallim's—no lions, no robbers, no Rephaites—just the occasional screeching of hawks and scurrying of lizards. The weeping maiden had convinced me Shealtah would be similarly in mourning, perhaps even perched atop a stool searching the hills for my return, and I hurried to ease the sorrow I was certain consumed her. But when I reached Dallim's familiar courtyard, the only signs of life were wisps from dinner's dying fire.

I tied my animals by the trough and was just about to enter the home when I heard a sudden gasp. Dallim had been reclining in the corner's shade, dozing off underneath his blanket when my presence startled him. He sat up with a start, sputtering and coughing as he demanded to know what I was doing there.

I answered him, "To see my wife, of course. I have brought along a goat for supper."

He looked perplexed and panicky, as if his mind were possessed of words his tongue could not form. Trying to regain himself with a sip of tea, the old man's hands shook so severely that most of the drink wound up splattered across his tunic.

When I walked inside and up the stairs, he jumped up and followed as fast as his old legs would carry him. "No! No, you cannot go!" he cried. He passed me and stood with his arms wide across the hallway that led to the bedrooms. I stared at him, not understanding.

While we looked at each other, I heard an odd wheezing. There in the great room, Schmealnah was sleeping on the couch. I tried to speak more quietly. "Father, you are the master of this house, and I respect you," I hissed. "But I am perplexed by your strange behavior. We can discuss it over chevon at supper. Please move out of my way, because I want to lay with my wife!"

He did not whisper when he answered: "Samson, I thought you hated her! You stormed off; you sent no word about your plans." He was pleading, almost flailing his arms. "What was I supposed to think? For all I knew, you had been killed by wild animals!"

"That will never happen, I assure you—"

"I was certain you hated her. You did hate her!"

"The day I left, I was angry. You know she exposed my riddle and cost me dearly," I said, my voice rising. "But the bitterness has expired. Now let me see her!"

I moved to pass, but the old man would not budge—bracing himself against the wall, he blocked me with the steely arm of a farmer and held me fast, shouting, "Listen and hear! I was so sure you hated her, I gave her to your companion—to Carillon."

"What?" I screamed, "WHAT?"

"Yes, to Carillon—your best man and good friend! He said you would have accepted this, and he is not particular about virgins—"

His words struck like a thunderbolt. I argued in disbelief: "Not particular about—he is not a good friend. He is not anything at all!"

"Yes, yes," he continued. "It was either Carillon or Maruck," Dallim mumbled, beginning to count on his fingers certain figures still in his head. "The priest's offer was…not reliable. Why, I should have been forced to pay *him*…" He came back to the present: "At any rate, Samson, they married a week after you left, once it was apparent Shealtah had displeased you.

What was I to do, I ask? What was I to do? She was promised a husband. You put her away! Since you rejected her, it seemed good to give her to a Philistine—"

"Dallim, say this is not so," I pleaded. "Say they have not been together." And I began to weep.

"Samson, Carillon pledged to work for his bride, and that he does! He bundled the vetch with diligence, and he has been a source of strength through the wheat harvest, too."

"That is the greatest deception of all!" I screamed. "The scoundrel is a lazy, deceitful jackal. He is a pathetic, fraudulent, self-serving louse. He's a rancid, conniving son of a—Gah!"

Then I came unbuckled and went berserk. I cursed Dallim and I cursed the Philistines. I cursed my engagement, my wedding, and that fat, racketeering, charlatan Maruck. I cursed sowing and I cursed reaping. I cursed the day I was born and every day since. But most of all, I cursed Carillon.

Dallim begged me to stop my tirade, but I was completely out of balance. I took one of his small bird statuettes and threw it against the wall, reducing it to a thousand shards. I pulled four legs out of a table and smashed the top over my knee. I yanked down a hanging urn, causing a dozen others to crash to the floor when the line snapped.

The commotion brought Shealtah out of her room to investigate—with Carillon in tow. Schmealnah continued sleeping, however.

"You!" I yelled, pointing at Carillon. "You stole my wife!"

"What are you doing here, Samson?" Shealtah asked, sounding confused. She looked…more plain than I remembered. Her hair was down and unkempt, and she wore an old smock. But when she laid eyes on me, there was neither happiness nor intimate familiarity in her voice.

"I came to see you," I cried.

"You left ages ago, Samson," Carillon interrupted. "It's like you told me that day: One man plows, and another comes and takes his harvest." And he smirked like we were old friends, because I do not think he understood my state.

"I should have fed you to the Nephilim!" I screamed, letting fly the urn still in my hand. The projectile missed his head by a fingerbreadth and broke through the lattice window behind him. I moved to punish him, and Carillon squealed in fear, cowering behind Shealtah. She and her father yelled at me to stop.

I raged against Carillon, that my family had cared for him, but he had caused us nothing but problems and pain. He argued like Dallim, that I left, and he thought I hated Shealtah, and that he would never have taken her if I had not left her. At this, she gave him a withering look that made me pause. I thought: She has none of the virtue of the mourning Israelite handmaiden—none of it at all. Moreover, as punishment for her faithlessness, she is yoked to a flatulent, careless weakling. That was just punishment for her betrayal. Meanwhile, Carillon would always know I had taken her first, not that such a thing bothered him.

He needed a throttling, and I intended to teach him a lesson that would mark him for life.

As I prepared to supply his beating, Dallim stood in front of me again, pleading for me to stop. Shealtah joined him, pushing against my chest to keep me away from Carillon. But together, they hardly slowed me.

With the two of them hanging onto my arms, I cornered Carillon, and was about to grind his face against the wall when Dallim stumbled backward into his feedbag stand. The entire thing tumbled over, scattering grain across the living room floor.

Such commotion at last awakened Schmealnah with a start. She sat up and looked at us positioned as we were, and we all stared back. Her hair was twisted and piled high like an uprooted tree, and she yawned and slowly wiped drool from her chin. "Samson?" she asked. "What was that noise?"

"It was the damned feedbags," I yelled, pointing to the floor where they spilled. "You might know something about feedbags, yes?"

"Oh, Samson," she said sleepily, lying back down with a smile. "You have not changed."

With arms outstretched and palms open, Dallim made to appease me: "Samson, isn't Shealtah's younger sister more attractive? Take Schmealnah to be your wife instead." It was the most crushing insult yet.

I looked at her, struggling to wake up, lying across the couch, and pondered the army of Philistines who had already had their way with her, including Carillon. I shook my head, laughing at his offer, then laughing longer—like a madman. Indeed I must have appeared insane.

"Yes, I will marry Samson," Schmealnah said to her father. "It is good to keep this Hebrew prize in the family, for he is very strong." She looked me over like one preparing to indulge in a delicious meal. "Samson," she said, "fetch your things and place them in my room."

For just a moment, a twinge of jealousy passed over Shealtah's face. Her eyes tightened, and she crossed her arms disapprovingly. Would it torment her if Carillon and I traded one for the other? Her sister was free for the taking if I was desperate enough. But a revenge marriage to Schmealnah? It would undoubtedly wear thin, probably before the night was passed. I looked at Shealtah again with anguish, staring to the point of awkwardness. She looked back at me, never breaking her gaze. But her sad eyes did not express any desire for me. Not for me, and not for a resumption of our marriage. She wanted me to leave. She had moved on, and she resolved herself to a life with that most odious creature, Carillon.

I continued staring at her and at them all for a time, and they stared back at me. At last I said, "I am leaving, and I am taking my goat."

As I walked out the front door, Shealtah called out, "Samson, wait."

I turned expectantly. At last she had come to her senses. She would join me and resume the life we had planned. Our eyes met, and she sighed. "Samson," she said, "if I never see you again, I will think of you on occasion."

Carillon shrugged his shoulders and agreed: "How could we not?" and Dallim nodded along. "This has all been *memorable*," he said. Schmealnah tilted her head and suggested the memories would be stronger if I left the goat.

I stared at them for a moment before moving to leave. Once out the door, a cloud of dust far down the road caught my eye. I looked to the trough: The goat was still tied, but the donkey was gone. I looked back to the road. Some Philistine rascal had stolen my ride, and he was at that very moment passing from view. What the hell is wrong with you people? When you aren't stealing from a family's pantry or staging a massacre, you seize a man's donkey! This—this was the final insult.

Anger and revulsion boiled over inside of me. I had half a mind to kill them all. I gnashed my teeth and let out a scream that made them flinch! Returning inside, I pointed to the date palms outside, speaking quietly at first: "These palms are a witness that I will not pass again to harm you. *But*," I cried, "do not dare pass them to harm me, or for any other reason. If I find you east of Timnah where the land rises, I will kill you! I will kill you where I find you, and your blood will be on your own heads. You have been fairly warned. Let God judge between us."

Shaking the dust from my tunic and sandals, I walked out with all hopes of marriage quenched within me, bringing to conclusion this awful portion of my life. I swore an oath on the spot I would remember this pain and never again let a woman entrap me with her love. But here I am, blind and chained, because I could not keep it.

That was the worst moment of my life. All of Carillon's repulsive boasting came back to me. The thought of him ravaging Shealtah night after night was more than I could comprehend. Though years and years have passed, my heart still cringes. The wound was worse than losing my eyes. It was an injury that cannot be healed, wrapped in shame that cannot be taken away. A good man who was suffering once said he knew his redeemer lived—and I share his hope—but I do not yet understand how even the mightiest redeemer can reduce such disgrace.

Chapter 30

Before my wedding, I had reason enough to hate the Philistines. Now I had a *right* to get even with them, and I determined to really harm them—but how? My rage demanded immeasurable punishment, yet my options seemed limited to a repetition of Ashkelon. Somehow, killing a patchwork jumble of Philistine wastrels, satisfying though it may have been, did not adequately convey the severity of my wrath. Before I had merely lost a bet; this time I had lost my helpmate and the vision of our future we conceived together.

All day, thoughts of revenge consumed me. But at night, as I lay there alone, visions of Carillon violating Shealtah—they left me bitter, angry, and despondent, beyond what mortal man can endure. Had I not made my oath before Dallim's palms, I would have returned to kill him.

How I pitied her, though: was Carillon what she envisioned when she desired a husband? Should the prize heifer be bred with a runt? What does it matter if he's of her own "kind"? In all the kingdoms of the world, I doubt one so fair was ever more unfortunately paired.

Nevertheless, Carillon was the one laying with her, and I was alone and heartbroken. My bowels were gripped with pain, and I began to waste away and look badly haggard. I refused to be consoled or to discuss the matter with anyone. My parents expressed concern, but I rejected their counsel— theirs and our village elders'. Didn't they all disapprove of my marriage to begin with? Yes, they did. And I knew what they would say. I would be forced to concede that every decision I made since I met Shealtah had come crashing down upon me like Abimelech's millstone. I did not need one of them or a Levite to tell me what I *should* have done, or to confirm my life had swerved off the path.

Because I had no peace, I took to wandering—here and there, to one boundary stone or another, up mountains, down streams—wherever the path led. What a picture of misery I was: a disturbed, sunken-eyed vagabond on a plodding journey to nowhere.

Early one morning, I traveled up through the foothills and sat down in the shadow of a broom tree, longing to be swept off the mountain. I lamented as I looked across the Valley of Sorek, to the Levite shepherds and their flocks at Beth Shemesh, and then to Timnah, the home of all my troubles. When I could bear it no longer, I turned away and cast my gaze upon Judah, where I spied a distant hill rising like a camel's hump, gently rounded and collared with vineyards. The sight moved me with a sudden longing like that of a restless caravaneer to "load wares" and see what might be seen from such a vantage. I set out immediately, descending into the valley, through the desert scrubland, past a handful of ramshackle villages before I reached the road to Kiriath Jearim in late afternoon.

In spite of the heat, this trek was no great hardship—I have always had rare endurance, and wells were plenteous along the way. Moreover, on the road my mind was released from Shealtah's grip. So when I ascended through the vineyards I had observed that morning, reached the summit, and took in the expanse of mountains before me, I thought: I should carry on. That was further confirmed when a mere look back toward my home filled my heart with pain.

Therefore, I continued down that slope and up the next, one after another, until the day was passed and the sun began to sink behind the western hills. As dusk settled on the valley,

I found myself alongside one of Judah's expansive wineries, when who should I pass on the road but my old friend Torgan. He was stopping up a fox tunnel into the vineyard with stones and mortar; he had also captured three yipping jackals and tied them on short leashes to a stake hammered into the ground. Their cries caused him much annoyance, and he would beat them into submission periodically with his catchpole—but their silence did not last long. By chance, he looked up as I approached, or else I would not have recognized him on account of the heavy leather skins he wore to protect himself from bites. When he saw me, he stood up and said, "Samson? Is that you here in Judah? I heard you were married. How are you, brother?" His brow furrowed. "You look…awful."

"Oh, Torgan, you would not believe what has happened," I said. Then I made him believe it with a thorough recounting of my pitiful misadventures: how I had met Carillon on the very journey home from the slaughter at Mahaneh Dan, and all about Shealtah and the other events that followed.

"What a night that was. Those damned Philistines," Torgan sighed. "You did such a kind thing for Isnach's parents. A beautiful thing, that. But your father took one of those deceiving bastards in—and he's nailing your wife? That's a hell of a payback, Samson, a hell of a payback. What are you going to do?"

"No revenge I have yet dreamed up is excessive enough. Many Philistines came to my wedding feast and took advantage of my parents' generosity. I would have them all pay—" About then, the jackals resumed their howling. Torgan cursed, turning to strike them, and I asked him, "Tell me, though, what are you doing with these?"

Between steady blows, he explained, "A lot of these rich Judahite vintners have trouble with jackals. They dig under the fences and eat the grapes before they are ripe. I have taken to capturing the little creeps to earn my bread. They travel in numbers, and I charge by the tail. For an added fee, I also stop up their tunnels and patch up the fences."

He finished abusing them and continued: "I sell them in Gath, where they know how to cook them just right. And I mean *just right*," he said, signing with his fingers. "Plus, they use the furs. Thus I do one job and collect two salaries."

That was the Torgan I knew—a good friend, and loyal, yes, but a schemer and conniver in the mold of our father Jacob. "Have you caught many?" I asked.

"Oh, you bet, Samson. Three here you can see, two dozen more you cannot at my parents' kennel. And if you would believe it, nearly a hundred more of these varmints are at my uncle's ranch halfway to Gath, near the Gibeonite encampment. Plus, he knows a Gittite butcher eager to buy."

As I sat there listening to his story and watching those frantic creatures squeal and yip and snap and fight to tear away, I became lost in thought. By the time Torgan asked me if my family had any trouble with jackals, I had just about worked out the details of a plan to do the Philistines as much harm as they had done me.

"Torgan," I interrupted, "I need these animals—and your skins, snares, and catchpole, too. Do not worry; I will pay you handsomely for them, for the tools, and for your lost income. I will reimburse you for it all."

He was surprised, of course, and reluctant, but when he heard my price, he agreed quickly enough, further conceding that I might use his uncle's holding pen (for a modest fee).

My countenance improved more during that portion of the conversation than it had since I learned about Shealtah's betrayal—even Torgan noticed, though it was mostly dark when we finished speaking.

I was lost in thoughts of hot, fiery vengeance when he said, "It is good to see you smile, Samson, in spite of it all." And I thanked him sincerely, feeling at peace with purpose for the first time in nearly two months.

Chapter 31

Over the next two weeks, I hunted high and low, far and wide, and wrangled every last jackal in eastern Dan, northern Judah and southern Ephraim. I brought them by fives and tens and twelves to Torgan's uncle until I had forty, and forty again, and forty more besides. They survived on a thin diet of pig and cattle carcass, or inferior kernels, or perhaps other jackals—I cannot say for certain as we did not inventory carefully.

Like men, the creatures were quick to coalesce into groups, to declare territory, and to nip at any who infringed. Predominant males took their harems, fights were frequent, and the noise was unbearable. If Torgan's uncle had not been old and half deaf, I am not sure he would have managed the blaring babble. On more than one occasion, Torgan's leather skins and catchpole saved me from a fierce bite, and maybe from the hydrophobia.

When at last I captured more jackals than I could hope to count, with the skulk on the verge of famine, the uncle demanded I unload the creatures to Gath for whatever amount I could generate, which I agreed I should do. But the time had come for retribution.

Once darkness fell, I corralled twenty or thirty jackals into a pullcart with a wooden lid. There was a small hole in the back, just big enough for one of them to exit, which I closed up. Hitching the load to two donkeys, I made for the nearby Philistine fields north of Gath. This was no long trip; the donkeys were severely disturbed by their cargo and made all haste, as if the jackals were biting at their hooves. Indeed, the creatures' constant, harmonized howling served as a more effective exhortation than the sharpest whip. They were louder than a throng of wailing women with tambourines, and I believe every Philistine farmer for miles must have thought it was a demon sorceress searching for a man to consume. Not one of them had the courage to come outside and see what the racket was about.

When I reached certain wheat fields about halfway between Timnah and Gath near the temple of Dagon where Maruck ruled, I used a rag doused in oil from the ferula root to lure the foxes out one by one, seizing their necks and tying them tightly in pairs by their tails. I put a loop in the rope and fastened in a fatwood brand, lighting it and sending them off like the desert sirocco. I reckoned each pair might run a hundred yards before they were roasted, causing catastrophic damage to Philistine crops, but certain pairs actually went much farther, doing even more harm than I hoped.

After these jackals were given their "warm farewell," I returned to base and gathered up a new cluster of the little devils, as many as would fit in the cart, releasing multiple loads in this same fashion in different areas around Ekron, Gath, and everywhere else the Philistines worked the land. By the tail end of the third watch, the entire sky glowed red as innumerable shocks of grain and acres upon acres of wheat, barley, vetch, peas, olives, and grapes all burned before my supply of fire carriers ran out.

Burn down my family's carob tree and barn, will you! Incinerate our barley sheaves! Raid the fruit of our labor! Who really carried the load of Seranim Occily's injustice? His thievery was repaid in full *that season* when the price of Israelite fruitage tripled in the five cities.

Late the next day, rumors began trickling in from Philistine territory that Sekhmet herself had arisen from Egypt to punish the Philistines for the sins of their fathers. Some claimed they had fled from her appalling cries, while others insisted her footprints had burned a pathway in advance of Pharaoh's hordes. The farmers lamented her fiery trail, darkly predicting of worse to come when the invaders arrived. They would have nothing left! Within a day or two, it was settled in the minds of most that this she-devil was absolutely responsible for the terrible devastation of their lands, and many prepared to flee from the invasion sure to follow.

The whole countryside was in an uproar, and Gath and the other Philistine cities closed their gates in panic. But when Seranim Occily demanded an explanation of the Egyptian envoy, the man swore on his life and the lives of his children that no such invasion was coming. Further, none of the people promoting this rumor had any sound information to share, only the ravings of fainthearted lunatics and conspiracists. All claimed they had heard news from their neighbors, such that the trail went in circles.

Consequently, the Seranim dispatched his sheriff to investigate further. Apparently, the man gave no credence to an Egyptian goddess on Philistine land, nor was he inclined to present the incoherencies of superstitious farmers to his master. But when he discovered charred fox carcasses tied in the same fashion in the various burn sites—usually with scraps of ashy fatwood nearby—he and his deputies made inquiries throughout the countryside, asking far and wide, "Who did this?"

By and by, they heard rumors of a fox catcher, a resentful Hebrew, and a misplaced wife, and—upon further examination of these accusations and putting the clues together—reported back to Seranim Occily it was "Samson, the Timnite's son-in-law, because his wife was given to his companion."

To learn more of these matters, the king dispatched his sheriff with a small detachment of soldiers to Dallim's property. Before they marched out of the city, rumors of the mission swirled about, and a large, vengeful crowd gathered to accompany them. By the time the procession arrived in Timnah, the rabble had grown exponentially, with many bad characters attached to the men whose properties had actually burned. They screamed for revenge and threatened violence, and the sheriff feared he and his men would be torn to pieces if they failed to carry out the mob's demands.

That damned scoundrel made a great show of questioning Dallim, who understandably knew nothing about the fires but everything about his daughter's remarriage. When the crowd heard that portion of the rumors confirmed, their bloodlust became unquenchable, and the sheriff allowed them to shout down every denial Dallim offered. They began to stone the old man, who was grievously wounded and bloody before he reached his home. It would have been better if he had died outside.

Rather than risk a riot, the sheriff determined to satisfy those murderous quarrelers around him. He barricaded Dallim's doors and windows with Shealtah, Schmealnah, and Carillon inside, and the crowd burned them all to death. They also stoned the old ape Pharaoh Ramesses when he came out to beg from the mob, and seized the remainder of Dallim's livestock and crop storage, each man stealing as much as his arms could hold.

About the time these Philistines were kicking up a cloud of dust on their way to Dallim's, a servant of my family's was also there, exploring a deal for millet because of a local crop failure. (Having washed his hands of the former dowry, my father hoped to renew minimal trade in spite of our prior difficulties. Dallim was at least a safer bet than Zilphah.) Unsure of the coming horde's intentions, but witnessing their angry cries and being already a Hebrew among enemies, our servant unhitched his cart and rode his donkey home at great speed.

We were eating dinner when he burst through the door, and when I heard his report, I jumped up and ran for Dallim's in spite of my parent's frantic protestations.

Long before I reached Timnah, I saw thick, black smoke rising high above the plain. By the time I could see Dallim's home, the smell of ash filled my nostrils. When I arrived, it was a mob scene. Looters were scattered about the ruins of the property, many with their hands full of produce or the family's relics, or else leading livestock one way or another. The first man I came across was exiting the property with three of Dallim's she goats, and he wore two heavy satchels filled with red grapes from the veranda. I grabbed him roughly, shook him, and demanded an accounting of events.

"Why are you assaulting me?" he snarled, pulling away angrily. "Go grab your share and leave me alone! Do you not know how this fellow was responsible for the great fires?" He was further cradling one of Dallim's hanging incense lanterns in rags, which was still hot from the house fire. I pressed it against his chest and demanded: "Where are the others? Where is Schealtah?" Though he screamed in pain, I did not relent.

"The fat one?" he cried. "Why do you care? She is burned to hell—let me go!"

"No, the thin one. The beautiful one! Where is she?"

"With her sister!" he yelled, squirming and fighting to get away. The commotion drew the attention of many other Philistines, who crowded around us and insisted I release the man, but I would not relax my grip.

As my eyes filled with tears, I asked them about Dallim and Carillon, too.

Some of them answered, "They also were burned on account of a Hebrew, who torched our land and destroyed our livelihoods! Are you the man?"

I suppose I realized then that I still held a measure of hope that my future would involve Shealtah, that I would somehow win her back. Indeed, I had reason to believe she and Dallim would choose me in short order over that pathetic weasel Carillon once they discovered how worthless he really was. While I did not mourn his passing for even a second—rather, I cursed the day we met—the suffering endured by Shealtah and the cold realization that I would never behold her again drove me to madness. She had betrayed me only to avoid the Philistines' threats of fire. How cruel that they burned her alive anyway.

Laying hold of my arms, the Philistines accused me a second time: "Well, how about it—are you the one who set those fires?" I stared at the ground, trembling and clenching my jaw. Gnashing my teeth, I growled in fury, "Yes, I am the man. And since you have acted like this, I swear I will not stop until I get my revenge on you!"

Then I shook them all off, broke the neck of the one I was holding, and smashed the burning hot incense lantern he had stolen over the head of another. A third man tried to help them, but I broke his hand, forced him down, and crushed his head with my heel. After this, the others screamed and scattered, most rushing back toward the smoking home where the sheriff and his soldiers were still bandying about. I went running toward them too, waving my arms frantically and yelling with the others to sow confusion.

The looters I ran with ran faster to escape from me, but I went right on yelling and flapping my arms with them, crying out, "He'll kill us all!" When they looked back at me, I looked back over my shoulder, and we all scurried pell-mell together up to the hill where several of the sheriff's guards were standing. One had drawn his sword to oppose an enemy he thought was chasing us.

"Get him, get him!" they screamed, but none of the guards saw clearly, because I screamed, too. When we reached the first guard, I grabbed his sword, wrenched his arm back, and cut off his head.

Two other guards stood with mouths agape, staring at their headless comrade. As they had not the sense to run or fight, I struck one down immediately and ran the other through, leaving the bloody sword protruding through his bowels for all to see. I seized their swords and began slashing at every Philistine I could reach. There was yelling and panic as wrath came upon them.

For his part, the sheriff at least comprehended his life was in danger. He ordered his armored men to form a line against me, but the Lord himself clouded their vision by calling forth a wind that wafted smoke from the smoldering fire among them, so they did not see me run behind Dallim's home. I slew two men who were rummaging around back there, snuck around the far side to the rear of the sheriff and his guards, and plunged into a crowd of Philistines cowering behind them. Some I recognized from my wedding party, and I hacked these apart with special gusto, striking here and there, smiting them hip and thigh with great slaughter.

Meanwhile, the armored guards had remained enveloped in smoke. At that very moment, though, the Lord put them into my hands when he dispersed the cloud to reveal their backs. I charged, stabbing one, slicing others, wreaking havoc, and rending them apart. On account of the smoke, these men did not have the wind to fight back. They were gasping for breath, coughing heavily, and their line was shattered. The survivors dropped their swords and ran for their lives with the rest of the Philistines.

The sheriff himself stood watching all this dumbfounded, scarcely believing a single enraged Hebrew could endanger his life. But mobs are fickle creatures, filled with rascals whose bravery is inspired only in numbers, who scatter as soon as a contest is in doubt. Thus as I approached, he found himself abandoned. Turning to run with eyes on me, he tripped over Pharaoh Ramesses' corpse and fell headlong into the water trough.

I was upon him in an instant; I stepped on his chest and forced him below the surface. He stared up at me, and I down at him, and I thought it fitting that he who murdered by fire would die by water, try as he might to raise himself. When the light extinguished from his eyes, I cried out to those few Philistines still within earshot, "I am Samson, and this is due vengeance for the murder of my wife!"

More than forty of my enemies were slain that day with the sheriff, including nine of his armored guards with their iron swords. Their corpses were scattered about Dallim's charred home as food for crows and leftovers for gutterpups. However, most of the mob escaped, and they would certainly fill Seranim Occily's court with demands for revenge.

Having declared my name and victory, I fully believed I had signed my own death warrant. But I hardly cared if I lived or died; only one thing remained. Ripping a large piece of cloth from the sheriff's wet sleeve to cover my mouth, I went to Dallim's front door and pulled away the ropes and boards the Philistines used to hold it shut.

Pushing in, I was immediately confronted by Carillon's charred corpse. What horror! Woe to all who die in fire. His hair and clothing, and the flesh on his legs, were all entirely burned away, and he had a bar fused to his hand. There were deep dents on the door's inner timber, and he must have fought until the end to save himself before succumbing to smoke and flame. Thus he died as he lived, with sole concern for his own skin; a wretched end for a wretched creature.

Dallim lay in the kitchen. While I did not grieve the old man, I did pity his conclusion.

Climbing upstairs, I made my way over scorched and warped floorboards, first to Shealtah's room, but it was empty. Smoke hung heavily in the burned-out husk of a home, and my eyes stung. I could hardly breathe, so I kicked open a shutter to let in light and air, but that rekindled the fire. As I continued searching, flames gained strength all around, climbing the walls and spreading across the ceiling. At last I found my beloved—in Schmealnah's room, in her sister's arms. The two were charred together in deathly embrace, and I…I wept. But I could not stay. The blaze was growing too intense. Even if it was not, I could not put her to rest as she deserved, because it was against my Nazarene vow.

I looked at her—burned to cinders—ashes to ashes.

By her knees on the floor was the small poppy-shaped silver broach, the same she had worn on our wedding day. With a cloth, I grabbed the trinket and walked out, broken and despondent. In this life, nothing beautiful is secure from the Philistines' rash injustice.

From a distance, I watched as the fire reemerged and the home collapsed to its foundation. Then I ran.

Chapter 32

There is a sense of final doom, bred through exhaustion and hopelessness, that draws desperate men to the cave called the Rock of Etam. Perched atop grassy, boulder-strewn cliffs in the Judean mountains, the Rock offers clear views of the northern and western highways below and—when the time comes—a rugged escape southward toward the Negev. When I fled from Timnah, I added my name to the rollcall of the condemned who have made the Rock of Etam their last refuge, before they are forced to a life of starlit wandering.

All was indeed lost, this I knew. I had come upon the Philistines in rage and swept away any who stood in my path, and this in plain view of a multitude of others. That these were already crying out for vengeance, I had no doubt. My only hope left was to draw the coming wrath far from my family. In case that too should fail, I sent word to my father with instructions to flee…to flee to…well, to a faraway place until all of this should come to pass—if indeed such events could come to pass.

All through the night I ran, with burning lung and blistered foot, not pausing for rest until I reached the crevassed foothills beneath the Rock of Etam, which is plainly visible by moonlight. The surrounding land is plentifully watered by streams, which make the area exceedingly rich with fruit and flower—a perfect hideaway for a doomed bandit.

For three days, I lay prone, pondering this new station in life. Henceforth, I would be a hunted man, in danger at all times, with a fat reward upon my head—one just as likely to tempt scoundrels among my own people as Philistine adventurers. Though still a young man, I must accept my status as a wandering widower in perpetual flight—the last stop on an irrevocable descent to Sheol, where there is no future but present darkness. The downward journey began with the massacre at Mahaneh Dan and now neared conclusion.

All my hopes were shaken to bits. There was no use trying to pick up the pieces and rebuild a life shattered beyond repair.

Yet, in truth, little of this bothered me, because my life was detestable to me. I was haunted night and day, whether in waking stupor or lucid dream, by Shealtah's miserable corpse. She was lifeless and ruined, crusted over in ash, seeking the comfort of her sister during a torturous gathering to eternity. To think of the pleasures and joys we experienced together… this final memory was branded onto my conscience, and—coupled with the shame of her remarriage to Carillon and the meaninglessness of days to come—drove me to a state of mania.

When at last I was overcome by hunger and could bear my fast and self-pity no longer, I emerged from my trance and made my way south to the village of Tekoa, rather than the nearer Bethlehem, to familiarize myself with the pass I must soon travel to escape.

In my wallet I had but a few coins, barely enough to purchase bread and oil from the caravansary. The outpost was well supplied in food and the people paid me no regard, neither showing hospitality nor persecution, but only dealing me a "Nazirite's glance" as I passed. They spoke freely of this and that, and thus I gathered word of my crisis had not reached them yet. None mentioned Samson or the Philistines.

I survived in the cave another two days on those rations. When hunger gained the best of me, I returned to Tekoa to revictual. This time, I found the mood in the town vastly changed. Worry shone in the eyes of every person willing to be seen in public, and many had already fled to the hills. The master of the inn had a particularly sour look on his bearded face, as his business was suffering. His bench was entirely empty save a basket of raisins and a scattered remnant of kernels and seeds, and he stared suspiciously at me with arms crossed.

"Your stock is quite sparse," I complained. "*Quite.*"

He answered unapologetically, "What do you expect? I am cleaned out."

I asked, "Do you have anything else for a half-shekel?" That was all I had left.

And he said, "Not much, and this is no time for credit."

I was very hungry and continued staring at his bench where the bread ought to have been. And he stared straight at me, as if he expected I would lift product that did not exist. His impatient scowl grew, and I began to feel an intense dislike for this man—if not for his cross cruelty, then for his wide-set eyes or weak voice, which choked with pain as he unfolded his arms and moved his hand to brace his back. "You ought to be going now," he said shakily. "The farmers and bakers are not delivering, what with the Philistines assembled in Lehi."

"I have barely eaten in two days," I answered. "Not since I was last here, and I cannot return home. Can you not spare any bread?"

Then his wide eyes narrowed, and he looked me up and down. "What do you mean, you 'cannot return home'? Where are you from? Why are you here?" he demanded. "Could you be the one the Philistines are searching for?"

I said, "I am sure of it. I slaughtered enough of them the other day. I am Samson, a Danite of Zorah, and I am undoubtedly the one they seek."

"A Danite? You *are* the one they are searching for!" he cried. "They intend to punish all Judah on your account. You can go and glean filth from the road, but I have nothing for you. If my back were not so sore, I would hand you over to them myself."

"You would do no such thing, you blustering fink. I slew forty men including the sheriff and his armored bodyguard with my own hands, and you would dare try to corral me? You cannot even corral a loaf of bread in your own shop—" and then, changing my tone out of desperation—"but even a stale crust I would gladly take, if you have one to spare."

"You will not take anything. Go home!" he said, slamming his fist into his hand, then grabbing his back again as he grimaced in pain. "Go bring wrath on your own community; we already have enough trouble here," he gasped. "Or better yet, spare us all and surrender yourself to the Philistines. I must go lie down."

"Well," I cried, "I cannot go and meet them on an empty stomach!" And I stormed out in anger.

On the way back to the Rock of Etam, I took a more westerly course and spent the afternoon gleaning millet from the edge of a large field with a handful of other vagrants. They were blissfully unaware that a man of desperate fate shared their space, and I wondered what it would be like to regain such innocence. Indeed, I envied their simple poverty. But such pondering is a fool's errand. A man must accept whatever fate the Lord assigns him.

Upon leaving the field, I found a wild sycamore fig tree nestled in a sharp valley. The tree possessed an abundant breba crop, and thus I returned to the cave well enough fed, though I would have preferred meat or baked bread for my "final" meal. With the Philistines mustering in Lehi, I knew my time was short. That cranky innkeeper would surely give me up, if he had not done so already. And I asked my God for peace and conviction for the trial to come.

While traffic on the roads had been sparse during my first few days in the Rock, by the next morning there was an unusual amount of activity below, including a handful of important-looking men leering up at me, pointing, and gesturing to each other, but they dared not approach. After a time, they hurried back from where they had come.

At about the noon hour, a body of men shockingly large, like an army several thousand strong, approached from the west. To my surprise, they were not Philistines. Unlike the "scouts" that morning, these fellows did not stop until they were within earshot of my position. They consisted of all manner of Judahites, plus a few leading men from other tribes, including my old adversary Macksam the Ephraimite, whom I threw into the stream with his companions before the slaughter at Mahaneh Dan. How he scowled when our eyes met! If he had his way, I knew my brothers would show no sympathy.

I came out to them and asked, "Why this delegation? Do you intend to harangue me altogether?"

The leader of the men of Judah was a grave man with sad grey eyes and a closely trimmed greying beard. Coming directly to me, he spoke up as the rest of the entourage continued walking up: "Samson, please. I am Benneson, son of Bennesor, of Bethlehem. Now we know you are dangerous, and that you executed the sheriff of Gath and his bodyguard. How you did this, we do not know. Will you explain it?"

"In a fair fight. They struck first."

The entire group stood silently, unsure of whether to argue or move on to a new subject, when Benneson cleared his throat and resumed: "That is not what the Philistines told us. Do you know why we are here?"

"Are you also running away?" I mocked. "If so, this cave is taken."

"We will ask the questions here!" Macksam shouted, barging to the front of the company. "Do you know the Philistine army is encamped at Lehi, or that they raided the city?"

"I heard rumors, but who can be certain in these dark times when a man will not defend his brother?"

Macksam's face turned bright red and spittle flew as he shouted: "Do not play the martyr with us, son of Bilhah. This army comes for you! You murdered the sheriff and any number of men besides. They have witnesses against you—many witnesses! There are enough to condemn you for your crimes." He gestured wildly as he made his speech.

"Would any of you bear witness against me?" I asked.

Macksam began to scream again, but Benneson shushed him, giving him a queer look that gave me flickering hope. He spoke slowly and carefully, though with the pain of inevitable loss: "Samson, none of us will bear witness against you, because none of us were at the conflict. But you know the Philistines are rulers over us. Do you understand that because you are here, rather than in Dan, they hold Judah liable for your actions?"

"I merely did to them what they did to me," I answered. "You need not provide security on my account—I have paid my debtors back in full."

"You see, I told you!" Macksam interrupted again. "He will never accept responsibility. You slop donkey, you dirty dog! You scoundrel, creeping in this desolate place like a slinking coyote. This time, Samson, you cannot throw everyone into the slough."

The elders all looked at him with uncertainty, but Macksam recovered quickly, arguing vehemently: "What I mean is, should his bounty be on our backs? Shall our children face judgment for his crimes? Let us strike him down and hand him over!"

I really thought they intended to kill me—clearly this argument had begun well before they arrived. Moreover, they had moved in and encircled me as we spoke, and the noose was tightening. Why had I let my guard down? And some of the men were armed. They might strike me down where we stood. What a fool I was, blindly assuming the Philistines were my only enemies.

But suddenly, a ram's horn sounded from below. And lo! There raced forward a magnificent sight—a small contingent of Machirites flying across the valley on horses like lightning, with banners waving and shield and spear flashing in the sun. We all watched in awe as they came to the place where the ground steepened and rode their steeds right up to our assemblage with shouting and another blast from the horn. Refusing to dismount, they barged directly into the circle of Judahites, scattering them this way and that.

It was an impressive display and a most welcome diversion from the present crisis.

Chapter 33

The Machirites are brave warriors, skilled with sword and bow, who share that old hero Johannon's vision of a free Israel—though they undervalue his conciliatory abilities. In those days, they wore orange and white tunics with purple turbans, carried banner and streamers, and spent all their time circling Mt. Hermon or on the outskirts of Gilead, battling raiders from Aram in the east and Philistine brigands in the west, one after another, until they either deemed an area pacified or else were chased away by a stronger force. They were led by a grizzled old warrior named Heshom and his sons, tall, cunning fighters who inspired immense devotion among their followers. When their numbers were depleted by enemies or loss of conviction, they never failed to recruit new desperados—men who loved to brawl, who had nothing else to lose. They cut down every foe mercilessly, taking neither prisoners nor slaves, and were a law unto themselves.

As their deeds became known, the Machirites were condemned throughout Israel for provoking Philistine vengeance, especially the massacre at Gibbethon. Even those who knew full well that injustice followed our enemies like fleas on a dog—like my parents, who understood intimately the brutality of the Seranim—were skeptical of this adventuring. The Machirites were especially despised by the wealthy, who resented above all else any risk to their abundance.

But I will say this on their behalf: When all the Judahites were determined to sacrifice me to the Philistines, the Machirites opposed them.

As I said, they burst through the line of men surrounding me and demanded an accounting of events. Heshom claimed they came as soon as they heard rumors of my fight with the Philistines. When he had it confirmed I had slain forty of the enemy, he gasped and praised me, "Like Nimrod, a mighty hunter before the Lord!"

Heshom proceeded to argue vehemently in my defense from atop his horse, telling the leaders of the Judahites, "I knew and admired your former champion Johannon. He was a great man—a man of courage, of action! But who are you? How can you condemn Samson when he struck down those who oppress your wives and children? We ought to pay him the Nephilim's bounty for slaying the sheriff of Gath, who was notorious for heaping misery on our people." And he condemned them all for cowardice and for submitting to the Philistine contingent when they were rallied together like an army themselves.

The Judahites did not know how to handle Heshom and his wild ones. They were humiliated by accusations against their manhood, pleading they had no weapons worthy of their heavily armed foes. But their disgrace had a readymade advocate in Macksam, a sharp-talking sure tongue, and he seized leadership of the entire delegation, stroking the pride of his allies: "The Philistine army has rallied here, in Judah— in the very heart of Israel!" He paused to let that sink in, looking dismissively at Heshom—"Far from *your* women and children, who are not at risk. And you ask these men to lose everything for the sake of one violent renegade. What do his crimes have to do with Israel's sovereignty?"

Heshom answered, "God alone is sovereign. But we are not all slaves. And *these*," he said, indicating three of the nearby riders, "are my children."

Macksam responded, pointing at me: "We are not all slaves *yet*—not so long as we make a prudent choice now. Is Samson Gideon, that he could lead you to victory against thousands? If so, go. We will not stop you." Shaking his head disappointedly, he said: "No, he is not Gideon. He is Abimelech, a reckless scoundrel with a drunkard's penchant for the fight. Yet a Nazirite! So what is his excuse?"

Heshom despised weak men like Macksam, and he had no patience for an extended debate. He sneered, saying: "You cry out like a woman scorned by her lover. What stake has Ephraim in Judah, that you would travel all this way to condemn this young man?"

Some of the younger Judahites looked up in awe of Heshom; with his sword and spear and his banners fluttering in the desert breeze, he moved them to reconsider their earlier intentions. But the older ones had more to lose, and they were entirely persuaded by Macksam, who sneered back at the warrior, "You ask what business is it of mine? I will return the question: What stake has Manasseh in Judah, that you should ride all this way in such a huff?"

Macksam turned away from Heshom, looking to Benneson and the other Judahite elders. "And for that matter, what has Dan against Judah, that this brawler would cause our enemies to muster here in force?" Pointing his thumb over his shoulder to his adversary of the moment, he said, "Should this horse rider and his band of brutes assume Jacob's promise from you? He envisions himself the fighting king of Israel!" He looked disapprovingly at Heshom's small group and spat. "You fools. Do you not see that it would be better for one man to die for your sins—*your* sins, you Machirites!—than for all of us to die for his?"

Heshom's eyes narrowed, his jaw clenched. "Do you not see, O merchant of Ephraim, if you concede one man to our enemies, they will insist on ten. And when you grant ten, they will take a hundred. To whom will you flaunt your wine and wares then?"

He continued to the rest: "For the span of our lives, we Israelites, who were granted liberty by God, have known only oppression. Are you no longer able to see anything better? Would Judah content himself with drinking from Philistia's muddy trough as long as he was allowed a pit to wallow?" And he spat back at Macksam.

Now, it was true that Macksam was already very wealthy in spite of his relative youth, but he had no interest in refunding Heshom's charges, for he saw clearly that enough of the Judahites already shared his determination to hand me over. Instead, he only scoffed. "An enemy sits encamped in force in Judah, and you want to preach like one of the Levites. Well then, unroll your scroll O wise Machirite: Show us who will save us from the Philistines *now*. The ten of you? You will scurry off to your mountain hideaway while our homes burn. Will God set a table for the rest of us out here in the desert?" There was a general murmur of agreement, and I knew Macksam had won the debate. My time was at hand.

Feeling his position strengthened, Macksam looked straight at Heshom—his voice rising in anger as he spoke: "You claim to champion Israel, yet would watch as our livelihoods were reduced to ash and our children sun-dried like raisins—for nothing! For less than nothing. For this oxen-headed ass. If you contend for this man's cause, you are no champion of Israel. You are not even a friend!"

Before he finished speaking, Heshom jumped down from his horse and unsheathed his sword. Macksam squealed and rushed to hide behind the Judahite elders, and many of them crowded between the two to prevent bloodshed, crying out that Heshom return sword to scabbard.

Benneson also stood between the two men and turned to the warrior, putting up his hands in a gesture of truce, wiping sweat from his face as he shushed the crowd. He said, "Peace brother," and offered Heshom a drink from his skin. But Heshom had a sense of the coming decision, and turned his back to him, angrily remounting his horse.

The Judahite stepped up upon a large stone and turned to address us all: "Men of Judah and Israel, and you Machirites, the Philistines are our enemies and we ought never to aid them. Nevertheless, they are stronger than we are. And we cannot allow our brothers, their wives and children to suffer violence when it is within our power to ward off more tragedy. Therefore," he said, nodding respectfully to Heshom, "though I am sure it grieves us one and all, Samson must submit to the justice of the Philistines, because he did not confront them on the battlefield, but in the yard."

Heshom pointed his sword at the Judahites, cursing them all as cowards. He urged them to "return to Egypt," that their wives might live in the safety of Pharaoh's harem. He saluted me as a hero, regretting he must leave before the smell of Judah's menstrual flow weakened him further. He and his men spat repeatedly, and they rode off in disgust. But Benneson and the other leaders paid him no heed. With the Machirites kicking up dust in the distance, Macksam resumed his calls that the safest course of action was to deliver my head to the Philistines, that they might be assured of Judah's commitment to peace.

Some agreed, but others protested, saying they ought not have my blood on their hands since I had not wronged them. I believe they were won over in part by Heshom. This caused Macksam to increase the vehemence of his arguments, until Benneson asked him, "Why this spite, Macksam? Do you hold a grudge against Samson? You know the Philistines claimed their rights to his life."

Up unto this point, I had not pleaded for my life, which I considered womanly. Macksam feigned innocence, putting up his hands and insisting he wanted only what was best for Judah and Ephraim. He refused to meet my eyes, which caused the Judahites' brows to furrow. I spoke up: "I threw him and his companions off a bridge into a muddy creek, and rightfully so, for they pressed us into carrying their luggage."

"I did not remember that until this very moment," he insisted, still not looking at me. One of the Judahites said, "No, Macksam—you never forget a debt."

Once they understood he was arguing for my execution out of malice, and would have swung a sword himself, they rightfully rejected his demands and said, "Listen, Samson, we have come to tie you up and hand you over to the Philistines. Are you willing to be handed over to them?"

I had not the heart for further arguing when the outcome was firmly settled. My eyes were downcast, and I said, "Swear to me that you won't kill me yourselves."

This they did, taking an oath they would tie me up and hand me over, but they would not harm me. That is why I submitted to their authority. Yes, they felt their hands were tied by the Philistine encampment at Lehi, but so what? They sold my life cheaply, and spent the purchase price on their own skins. These so-called men lacked the stomach for fighting, and sacrificed honor to preserve what little comfort they had. Therefore, my bitterness against Judah lingers. It lingers to this very day.

Two of the younger men took rope from one who hid himself in the crowd and came to tie my hands and legs. Their rope was still white, thick and strong without any snag or tear, and Macksam approached with an explanation: "The

Philistines gave us new ropes to bind you, Samson. Make no mistake: you will take the bit. You will take it and chew it until your teeth shatter, because your hour for breaking has at last come."

Chapter 34

What a grand procession we formed, a condemned man and three thousand fainthearts hiding in his shadow. Though the sun was in our eyes and I was bound hand and foot, the Judahites forced me to shuffle along at a brisk pace because they were eager to settle the matter before the Philistines reached the end of their rations. How I regretted my peaceful submission. I thought: if only I could die fighting, I would be content to take even one more of the enemy with me.

Our parade carried on in ashamed silence until I heard Macksam suggest we ought to sing a dirge of remembrance for a soon-to-be-forgotten man, but no one humored him, and he kept quiet thereafter. No one said a word of comfort to me, either; no one offered any kindness or hope. The ropes made it difficult to tread the steep and rocky places, but when I stumbled, no one offered his hand.

At the Eltekon crossroads, our convoy crossed paths with a bright young Levite of no more than ten. The boy traveled with his mother, and his name was Samuel. When he discovered our errand, he left her and joined with us, insisting he be allowed to speak with me. Sidling up quietly, he offered a bite of the saltiest goat jerky I ever tasted. My face puckered, and I glared at the child and said, "This is the cruelest betrayal yet."

He frowned and continued eating off the meat, as if to show he meant no harm. Between bites, he asked if there was anything he might do for me.

I said, "Yes. I need you to help me escape."

His sideways glance gave away faint disapproval. "Brother," he said, "when a man faces certain judgment, he ought to consider very carefully his words and his ways. He ought to prepare an accounting of his life."

These were not the words of a boy, and I understood right then he was no ordinary child. Yet in my bitterness, I continued antagonizing him. "Thank you," I said. "That is very comforting. Truly, you are a worthy heir to Aaron, for you have inherited his gift for eloquence."

Samuel looked questioningly at me and shook his head. "What can I say to you that would help? You are determined to make a fight of it."

"I only wish I could! Here I am, bound by my brothers and led like a lamb to dishonorable slaughter. I have become a scapegoat for these Judahites. Where is *my* scapegoat? I need a scapegoat of my own. Instead a child is my only comforter."

We walked along in silence for another moment, and he twirled his forelock around his fingers and rubbed his smooth chin thoughtfully. Looking up at me, he said, "The Lord is a redeemer; he can redeem you with his mighty outstretched arm—"

"Yes!" I interrupted. "And where is the Lord? What about his mountain of fire and his tower of smoke? Where are his miracles, his promises, and his almighty power?"

Samuel looked at me queerly, as if he were searching for words that should have been obvious to all. He stopped and put his arm on my shoulder, and the men behind us stopped, too. "Samson," he said, "I must get back to my mother and be on my way. But I will tell you plainly: You are asking the wrong questions. You ought never ask, 'Where is God?' as if he owed us an accounting of his presence."

"Well, what *ought* I to ask of the Lord on my way to Dagon's altar?"

"The answer is as old as Adam, and was tendered the man after his indiscretion: 'Where are *you?*' Yes, where are you."

As the Judahites grumbled to "drive on" and nudged me forward, I told Samuel, "I would like to be with him, or else anywhere but here."

"You do not understand," he said sternly. "The Lord is with you, Samson. *Are you with him?*"

Moving off the path, he climbed atop a small boulder and waved goodbye as I carried onward. "May the Lord be with you, Samson," he called. "And may your *heart* be fully with him." With that, he reversed course and went on his way.

For the next several hours of this miserable journey, I considered Samuel's rebuke. Slowly, I found myself persuaded by the Levite child, in spite of his youth. I had a change of heart, and repented of my sin and disinterest toward the name of the Lord. I called on him: "Lord, whatever becomes of me, may my mind and heart be wholly with you. May my strength and endurance be of you. I am your servant." And I felt a small measure of peace that grew with each passing step, in total contradiction to my wretched circumstances.

The sun fell to the horizon and the sky turned red.

By the time we reached the plain at Lehi, the parade of Judahites behind me had diminished to a few dozen men, the rest having returned home once they were assured of Philistine satisfaction. As we approached the enemy encampment, the remainder of my entourage scurried off, until only three remained—Benneson and two others behind him, armed with iron swords! So, the Judahites had personally escorted a contingent of Philistines.

Benneson said to them he had fulfilled their master's demands, and I understood all. My anger grew hot, my heart raged.

The Philistine guards were joined by multiple sentries from the edge of their camp. These led out a hostage on a donkey, who gathered up Benneson.

"Farewell, son of Bilhah," he said as they hurriedly departed. I turned for a last look and stumbled over a stone. The Philistines accused me of cowardice and threatened to make my ending very much worse if I did not hurry along. They wore the black armor of Gath's elite guards, the so-called "Red Bolts," marked with blood-red lightning. One of them struck me with the flat of his sword on the back of my thigh, and it stung badly.

As they marched me into the center of their camp, the whole army raised such a cry that you would have thought Pharaoh himself had come to pay obeisance. They all put down their plates of donkey flesh and gathered around to jeer me, asking if I still felt like a big man. They called me a damn Hebrew dog and an ugly rat-faced bastard—which was not true. In those days, I was one of the best-looking men in all of Israel, and everyone said so. They heaped on many other crude insults typical of Gittite soldiers: That my mother was the sort of whore who had to pay for customers, my own testicles would be my final meal, and so on.

The guards dragged me along roughly before their commanding officers and flag bearers, who stood expectantly alongside a hastily constructed altar to Dagon with his priests atop a small hill. I recognized there my old foe Maruck, who stood quietly as unto his rank. When our eyes met, he shook his head slowly and ran his thumb across his neck.

The commanding officer raised his hands to silence his troops, who all circled round. I recognized this scoundrel, too; he was the very same that led the ransacking of my family's property shortly before my marriage to Shealtah.

When he spoke up, he scanned his men and said, "Kanus, where are you?" A stout soldier moved slowly forward and presented himself, gnashing his teeth as he turned to face me. "Yes, I believe Kanus wanted to address our guest first. Let us give him the honor. It is about a matter of family justice as I understand it."

This "Kanus" fellow had his hair pulled back tightly and his beard cut to a point, and he came up and stared at me long and hard. He was of good size and make, with an arrogant look in his eye—as many men will when they are confronting a subdued foe. He drank lustily from a large chalice and spat wine in my face, eliciting a cheer from his brothers. Then he threw down his cup and cursed me, ripping off my tunic. I stood there facing him—facing them all—alone, in only my undergarment, but I held no fear. The Lord kept me.

Kanus did not speak. He just continued staring at me, well past the point of awkwardness. At last I took an attitude and said sharply: "Well?"

He answered, "The sheriff you murdered was my uncle. One of his bodyguards was my cousin. Now I am going to do you worse than you did them." Sticking his finger in my chest, he added, "If you knew what was coming, you would beg—*beg*—for the indignity of drowning in horse's spit." And he drew his sword slowly and deliberately, without ever breaking eye contact.

Kanus moved closer, and the other soldiers crowded round and urged him on, crying out, "Carve him up!"

This now—*this* was the moment of judgment. But it was not the judgment Kanus or any of the Philistines expected. It was not *I* who was judged! Ha ha! Because the Lord—the Lord God Almighty—saw fit to vindicate me and to break the yoke of the Philistines. And no gouging of eyes can change who proved best that day.

As Kanus moved in for the kill, suddenly a powerful wind blew through the camp. I cried out to the Sovereign Lord, and the Spirit of God came over me. New strength poured into me, coursing through me, needing release. I flexed and tore apart my bindings as if they were nothing more than charred flax. The Philistines watched in amazement as their new ropes disintegrated and blew away like chaff. But that Kanus, he had no panic in his eyes, either. Indeed, I think he relished a fight. Taking careful aim, he swung at me such a blow that would have shortened me by a head, but I ducked and rolled away.

Next to the campfire was a heavy jawbone of an ass recently filleted by the invaders and picked clean by birds. Perhaps it was the one stolen from me at Dallim's. I scooped it up and assumed a defensive position against Kanus. None of his brothers believed he could lose; they found our sport entertaining.

He lunged at me again and again, but each time I dodged his attacks, and my confidence grew. Spurred on by his comrades, he grew impatient in his charge and thought to hold his blow, to catch me on the back foot. It was a fatal error. When he came at me again and feinted a strike, I dealt him such a thumping with that jawbone that his skull broke in and his brains poured out.

There was a gasp from them all. The nearest guard stood staring open-mouthed, asking dumbly, "But how did you tear the ropes?"

And I answered him with a square shot across the mouth, busting his chops so his chin aligned with his ear. He fell into the fire, and the whole camp filled with the smell of burning flesh before they pulled him out.

I taunted the Philistines, "Is there not a man among you to challenge me?" for I thought, better one at a time than all at once.

A large fellow answered the call and came forward with a spear. Though he was adorned in the breastplate of a champion, his charge lacked conviction. I dodged the spearpoint and grabbed the shaft, standing this "bolt" straight up and striking him in the temple. The blood spurted out and he fell hard. While the Philistines watched, I pinned their champion to the earth with his own weapon.

The next nearest man was the guard who struck my thigh on the way into camp, and he loosed his sword. Before he attacked, I broke off the butt end of the spear and threw it like a javelin into his stomach. The man doubled over in mortal pain, and I bashed him over the back of his head down into the dust. Standing straight up with chest out, I turned slowly, facing the Philistines all around. Four of their own lay dead already in this makeshift desert arena, but many more were to follow.

"Now," I said, flipping the ass's jawbone from one hand to the other, "who is ready?"

Chapter 35

But you are certain you want to hear again the next chapter of this tale? How the pride of the Philistine army was ground into the desert rough. What can you hope to uncover that has not already been told? The spectacle was well established even among your own record keepers, confirmed by the Israelites who bore witness to the fight, the Philistine grave diggers, and the despicable one who escaped. Are not the Red Bolts mourned each year during the wheat harvest, when their banner is unfurled in solemn remembrance before the Seranim and his officials in Gath?

You want to know if I ate a magical root perhaps, or some other desert herb infused with strength. Ha! No, I tell you, the power is in the power, and the power belongs to the Lord. It was his hand that struck the Red Bolts.

Ah, the Red Bolts—they made their name at Kadesh when they turned over Hatti's iron chariots. But in the badlands against Samson, their mighty deeds came to an end...

As I was saying, four men lay dead before me, and the Philistines stared in shock and horror and grief. But these feelings faded quickly enough to blind fury. These were, after all, Philistia's most battle-hardened, decorated soldiers—men who "struck like lightning" and drenched the earth with the blood of their enemies, or so it was said.

Awaking from their stupor, they drew their swords, raised their spears, and cried out in such a rage that I knew the fight would begin for real.

They rushed at me from all sides like a mob, rash and reckless, driven by anger and the shame of seeing their own slain by a man in his underwear. Yet they had none of their famed martial shape to speak of, no discipline, and they tripped over each other in their determination to get at me. The spearmen could not lower their weapons on account of the crowding swordsmen, who thought they deserved first go—much to the aggravation of the slingers and archers, who were forced to put away those weapons for their knives. In the din of close quarters combat, their commanding officer's orders went unheeded, and he was reduced to cheering them on: "There he goes—hit him," or "Strike him down; this is your chance," or at last, "Kill that damned Hebrew!"

I, however, faced nothing so confusing as an incompetent officer's orders, nor any cause for hesitation at all. I struck with abandon and my aim was true. With such a crowd surrounding, how could I miss? In a frenzy of violence and death, I battered their heads and necks and struck at their faces where there was no armor. Every blow found its mark, and those I hit no longer lived. Their helmets bent and shattered, and the dead piled up thick around me.

With forty or more men down, the Philistines kept coming. They could not read the signs, perhaps because each saw little more than the man in front of him as they pressed around me, or maybe they could not accept that a ruffian with the jawbone of an ass was routing the best of them.

Whatever the case, whether pride or idiocy, when the officers understood their men were being massacred, they panicked and shouted all the louder, "Kill him! Kill him now!" I suspect they feared returning to Gath with a depleted regiment and an impossible defeat—and certain execution. Thus, failure was multiplied tenfold into catastrophic destruction and the end of Philistine rule over Israel. As the commander ordered his soldiers headlong into slaughter, I determined he also should have no right of return. But that pilferer's time still had not yet come, though it was very close.

As I slew his men in heaps upon heaps, he gathered a line of spearmen in reserve—though I did not know it at the time. These he moved up behind the soldiers who had me occupied, where I danced between thrusts and leapt over the fallen, battering one, busting another, reducing them man by man. From one I seized a shield made all of hammered copper.

The commander quietly ordered his spearmen to charge. I might not have ever known they were rushing forward if not for fear in the eyes of my present foe. I jumped and spun to face this cowardly rearward assault as he was run through by one of his own!

Had I not upraised the shield, my fate would have been no different. A half-dozen iron spear tips struck at once, but the copper held true—though I was knocked backward over a pile of Philistine dead. One of the attackers snuck his spear past my shield, in between my right arm and ribs, which drew a gush of blood from either side. He cried out, "We've got him now!"

But he was wrong. I somersaulted back, leapt up, and let fly the shield on its side like a disk right through the center of the enemy's line. It struck the two spearmen there square in the face, shattering their jaws and laying them out for good. I ran through the gap before their comrades could close ranks, and beat their brains out—close in, where their long spears were of no use.

A handful of the living rallied to reform their line—maybe three or four. Not many of that group were left. They raised their weapons to charge, but I heaved one of their brothers atop their outstretched spears. Before they could shake him off, I pounced, buffeting them down into the dust.

Next, I—but really, shall I go on? The look in your eyes reveals your pain. Do you want to hear how the rest of the

Red Bolts came unto extinction? Is it not painful for you? The story only repeats itself again and again, until the army was entirely reduced.

Therefore, I will conclude with a final memory. After the last of those spearmen was dispatched, the Philistine commander cried out, "You son of a bitch! That was my son!" He came at me with sword raised, but I easily sidestepped his blow, and he stumbled over his boy. I stood over him with jawbone raised; his face shown no fear, and he said, "Now I know where I have seen you before—" but I did not allow his remembrance. I turned his face into a bowl for soup. Thus, he was justly repaid for stealing from our harvest and burning our property before my wedding.

To their credit, the Red Bolts fought on and on admirably, in spite of their mounting casualties and the loss of their leaders.

Until that time, I had not a moment to reflect on the nature of this fight, or to consider I might survive; my sole focus was to kill. But I began to have a sense the day was won when I saw the peaks of the Judean Mountains glowing fiery orange in the sunset. Before then, the Philistine ranks were far too thick to comprehend anything beyond the man in front of me. Now, the dead were winnowed into heaps and the handful of survivors scattered in disarray.

Yes, I crushed them all, until their carcasses lay in piles eight or ten deep. It was fourfold revenge for the murders at Mahaneh Dan with another measure besides.

And I will say this: If the Judahites possessed any measure of courage, they might have shared in my glorious victory and assumed the rulership Jacob prophesied. Instead, God gave me sole mastery of the Philistines, and that with the jawbone of a donkey—heaps upon heaps. With the jawbone of a donkey, I slew a thousand men.

Chapter 36

My abiding memory of that contest is not what you would think, for I felt no rush of victory, no surprise that God had delivered me from so overwhelming a foe. Nor did I have any regard for the demise of Philistine oppression. The meaning of this story was of little concern to me.

What I remember most vividly was an all-consuming thirst. I had still the irritation of that Levite child's salt meat in my mouth, and I thought—*woe to me.* I have survived sword and spear, but will be undone by goat jerky! My tongue swelled and my throat burned.

As I watched the contingent of Philistine survivors scurry off, I threw away the jawbone and dropped to my knees. My face hit the dust, and it clung to my chapped lips. I panted to the Lord my God, barely able to mouth my plea: "You have granted this great salvation by the hand of your servant, and shall I now die of thirst and fall into the hands of the uncircumcised?"

Looking again, I marveled that the jawbone had landed in a small hollow, and lo! It glistened. I retrieved the weapon and sucked water out, then collapsed to the ground to drink my fill from the pool. My strength returned, and I praised God for his mercy. If old Gideon had seen me, he would surely have hired me on, for I plunged my head down into the hole like a dog.

Only once I revived did I begin to understand this was a victory as from days of old, like one the Levites teach the children about. Indeed, one of the priests later told me my triumph was the fulfillment and surpassing of Moses' prophecy, that five men should conquer a hundred.

As I stood and surveyed the destruction around me—the Philistines' best young warriors slaughtered, with their heads all beaten in—at that very moment, I heard again the same ram's horn from earlier, and in the distance the cries of battle. I climbed atop the altar to Dagon the Philistines had constructed, and sure enough, Heshom and his warriors were riding down hard on the last of the Red Bolts, determined to keep any from escaping. Silhouetted against a blood-red sunset, they rode rapidly around the enemy, forcing them to gather together in a tight circle bristling with spears—though the Machirites were, in fact, smaller in number.

Around and around the horse riders went, until one of the Philistines became unnerved and lunged at a Machirite. That rider veered out of the way and the attacker was quickly speared by the ensuing horseman. Before the enemy could tighten their circle, another rider dismounted like lightning and fired a deadly arrow into the cluster. One man fell, the circle broke, and every remaining Philistine dropped his weapon and ran for his life. But being on foot, they had no hope of escape. Heshom and his riders chased them all down and dispatched them mercilessly. Thus the last of the Red Bolts came to a final, complete annihilation.

While his two youngest sons ensured each Philistine was dead, Heshom and the others rode to me. With mouths agape, they reviewed the heaps of dead Philistines, until at last Heshom said, "Hail, mighty warrior of God!" They looked at me closely in amazement and asked, "Has the Sovereign Lord really given you, and you alone, this victory?"

"He has," I said. "By my hands, he has inflicted judgment and vengeance on the enemy. With the jawbone of an ass—" which I raised to show them "—I made an ass of them all.

On this day, he has avenged his servant in full, even down to the donkey that was stolen from him." And I dropped the jawbone.

Heshom and his men cheered. They dismounted and bowed low, clothing me in one of their robes since I still appeared there in my underwear. And he said, "Behold this viper who slays the Philistine invaders and delivers justice for all Israel. Gideon had his 300, but you have prevailed against your enemies alone. We will always remember our champions of old, but the time has come when Israel's children will sing of you first!" He picked up the jawbone covered in blood and brains and swung it forth, showing it to his men as he spoke quietly, "The weapon of God's judgment."

Heshom turned to me, and handing over the jawbone, said, "Young lion, do not neglect this prize; it is the trophy the Lord awarded you today, and a headstone for your enemies." He looked back to his men and spoke longingly, "With this jawbone, we shall rally armies of Israel and throw the Philistines back into the sea."

I squinted at Heshom, but he continued: "What do you want now, Samson? What do you intend to do?"

"I would like to get a new donkey," I said. "Some Philistine rascal stole mine."

They were perplexed. "Yes," Heshom stuttered. "We will see you get a new donkey. But what are you really going to do? Will you begin in Dan? Or would you set up camp in Gilgal? Or Shiloh?" He saw my questioning disapproval and guessed again: "Mizpah? Only order your servants to call forth the Israelites in your name."

"I hear your words but do not understand their meaning," I answered. "My servants are not heralds—they are fruit pickers. And I intend to return to my property for the harvest. There is much to be done this time of year."

Heshom gave his men a queer glance before looking back to me. "Surely this is no time to jest."

"No, the fruit of my family's labor—"

"Samson, my son," he spoke up, taking off his turban. "Grapes are a pittance. Would you make wine or raisins when you could make a nation?"

I said, "No, I am a Nazirite. I have sworn off—"

"I understand all that," he interrupted impatiently. "What are *you* talking about? The harvest—*any* harvest—is a pile of horse droppings. Do you not see that? Do you not see what is at stake? What we are talking about, what you and you alone can achieve, is the fortune of leading your people to victory. Of securing our birthright inheritance and fulfilling God's promise." His voice was growing in passion and excitement: "Lead us to victory, Samson, and something greater than a harvest will find you. Wealth and success will come to you. Just try to hide from them! You will not succeed. Your grains and fruits and nuts would in no way begin to tip the scales against such prizes, I assure you!"

"Pha! Do you not remember this morning? Judah sold me out to save their own skins. Thousands of men, and not one willing to pick up a sword. It has been given to Judah to rule, but they will not have me. And that damned Macksam—he is wealthy. He will ensure no Ephraimite lifts a finger."

Heshom shook his head and hit his hand to his fist: "Macksam…I should have killed that scoundrel merchant. But look, Samson: this morning, those Judahites were the wealthy men—leading men, men with much to lose. There are many others who will support you, if only they are led—" He looked to the iron weapons scattered around, and continued: "If they are led, and if they are armed. Look around you. You have earned an armory! Iron swords, leather armor, spears, helmets."

One of Heshom's sons, named Habnoch, chimed in: "And a woman, Samson! You can take a new Hebrew wife—"

His father silenced him with a sharp look, but I laughed bitterly. "Look at the dead piled around you," I said, shaking my head. "If a foreign woman should cause such strife, what then a Hebrew?"

Habnoch argued: "Would you hide at home—"

But Heshom interrupted. "Samson, forgive my young son, though he is older than you. In his *ignorance*—" and he glared hard at Habnoch, "—he spoke of things he should not. In truth, this moment is not about women or wealth or any other carnality." And he paused and resumed glaring at his son before at last proceeding: "Samson, God is with you. *With you*. And we are with you. For forty years, the Philistines have heaped misery and injustice on our people. Our children have never known anything but oppression."

He continued: "I remember the days of my youth, when we lived without fear of the Philistines. And I remember when that fear arose. What started with petty thievery and unwarranted beatings spread like a shadow across our land with seizures and burnings and murder and rape. Darkness had come, such that many people still have no hope of light. They have no vision.

"You and you alone can change this story, Samson. The spirit of God is upon you. Around you are the mandatories of Israel's salvation. Come back with us to Gilead, and let us gather men to join you. Or else go to the tabernacle at Shiloh. Only choose where you would establish a base, and Israel will rally to you."

Until that moment, it never occurred to me that I would lead Israel. But God raises a man for his purposes, and lowers him—as surely as you see me now lowered. The Machirites urged me to go with them for a while longer, but the sun set and I grew exceedingly tired. Heshom's sons set a table and we ate, praising God for my victory and continuing our discussion. Through the course of dinner, my companions' arguments won the night. I had no cause to doubt them. After all, they had done everything they could to save me from the Judahites and Philistines, committing also to gather my body when they feared my doom, to save me from the disgrace of unburial or base defilement. And they had risked their lives and shown their skill in dispatching the Philistine remnant, who outnumbered them at that.

Therefore, I was persuaded, though I could not discuss the matter further. I said, "I am tired and must lay down my head. Even Jacob's pillow would I gladly borrow, if only I can rest. In the morning, I will go with you. But let me sleep, because I am worn to exhaustion."

They set up Heshom's own tent for me, but they themselves kept awake for many hours, drinking hot tea and marveling at my God-given victory. Later they slept around the tent like a bodyguard, in case any of the Philistine dead were not so dead as they seemed.

As for me, for the first time since I left Shealtah, I slept in peace. The destruction of the Philistine army was more than fair reimbursement for my broken marriage and slain wife, and I felt closure beside the heaps upon heaps of their dead.

Chapter 37

When I finally emerged the next morning from Heshom's tent, his sons had already removed most of the Philistines' armor and sorted their weapons. I joined them, and we tore down the vile altar to Dagon and left our waste upon it. Thus was another of the Rephaite's sins at Mahaneh Dan avenged, when they tore down and defiled the altar to the Lord.

The Machirites proceeded to circumcise the dead. I thought, it is a little late for this covenant!

But Heshom had sound reason for the exercise, as indeed he always did. At dawn the following day, he appeared a solitary figure at the main city gate of Gath. Blowing his ram's horn, he cried out to all who could hear that the Red Bolts were come to their end on the plains of Israel at the hands of a new champion. Not one man was left, he said, presenting their banner, foreskins, and the head of their commander as proof of his claims. He wiped his feet on the banner and delivered an ultimatum, that Israel had broken free of the yoke of the Philistines. There would be no further seizures, collections, kidnappings, murders, pillaging, or anything else of that sort. Any Philistine who carried a sword into Israel, whether alone or with ten thousand others, would face the same judgment as the Red Bolts and be summarily slain without hope of mercy.

Moreover, Heshom demanded a small contingent of Philistines come with wagons to collect their dead lest they be left as carrion for vultures. He guaranteed safe passage for this train, and said they would be escorted by two of his men on horseback—just as two Philistines traveled with the Judahites when they confronted me. This was carried out a day later.

The Machirites went on to press some of the Philistine villagers to set up new boundary stones on the eastern side of Gath, where no Philistine warrior should pass lest his blood be upon his own head. He also crushed to gravel the dressed stones the Philistines had prepared for Dagon at Lehi as an act of insolence against that false god.

Fear and sorrow overwhelmed Gath that day and for some time afterwards; indeed, Heshom said he began to hear wailing from his position outside the city walls. When the Philistines confirmed the head returned belonged to the Red Bolts' chief, Seranim Occily tore his clothes and ordered his nobles to mourn for thirty days, and all the people with them. Gath levied raw soldiers from Ashdod and Ashkelon, but they were kept within the walls. Fear of God had come upon the city.

A week later, the gates were reopened for the first time and my enemy Maruck made his way in to the council of lords, where he offered a mostly accurate accounting of events. He lied only in this respect: To hide his cowardly flight, he claimed I rendered him unconscious with a blow, and the dead piled on top of him. This was false; I never struck him. I would have savored that conquest and made doubly certain he was dead, since I held him chiefly responsible for the breaking of my riddle and the end of my marriage.

At any rate, he escaped in the middle of the night after playing dead, scurrying off to the northeast rather than the straight westward path to Gath for fear he would be ridden down in the morning.

While all of this was taking place, I sent word to my parents through one of Heshom's riders to return home, where I soon met them. I had not seen or spoken with them since these troubles all began at Dallim's with the fire, and they knew nothing of my whereabouts or circumstances. Listening in awe and wonder, they praised God for the fulfillment of the prophecy of my birth, which they revealed to me in full. Previously, they had kept the matter private because they did not want to burden me with visions of confrontation before the Lord's appointed time.

My young brothers looked up to me in awe. They went on to brag to their friends that I was the strongest in the world, that I beat out all the Philistines, and that I would beat them out too if any disagreed.

I told my parents of Heshom's urging to go with him and secure Israel, but not of my watery commitment to actually do so. I offered to stay with them instead to complete the harvest, reminding them of my indebtedness to their purse on account of the failure of my marriage to Shealtah. Much to my surprise, they vehemently opposed this plan, agreeing wholeheartedly with Heshom that I should go, that God had raised me for just such a time as this, and that a return to the orchards was absurd after such a mighty victory.

Their words relieved the burden of one conviction and strengthened the other, and I thanked them with tears. My father teased me and said it was no coincidence that the first time I accepted his advice was the one time it took me away from my responsibilities. Later, I heard he had begun telling his associates, "Samson is so stubborn, he refused to be killed by a Philistine army."

Though my brothers begged to come, my father rebuked them gently, insisting they "wait for their time, just as Samson did." The three of them jumped on me and we wrestled, and I let them overcome me until they claimed they were the strongest under heaven.

As with my returning Isnach's body or my engagement to Shealtah, news of my victory over the Philistine army spread rapidly. Indeed, it became a cause of praise and musical celebration throughout all Israel, and led many to return to the Lord our God. My parents began to speak publicly of their encounter with the Lord's angel before my birth, and the people accepted I was born for wonderful purposes.

Meanwhile, Gath, being the nearest of the five cities and the spearpoint of Philistine abuse against Israel, grew exceedingly quiet. With its best soldiers tamed, oppression ceased. For a time, Seranim Occily dared not allow any to cross Heshom's boundary stones. Of course, it was inevitable that scroungers and raiders would come, quietly at first, and then in a torrent (but those stories in their proper time), because his people had ruled over Israel and could not accept such a role reversal. Without others to look down upon, they were forced to consider their own miserable lot in life. Military disasters were easier to accept.

The following morning, I left for Mizpah, where I was welcomed with flowers and feasting, with kisses from pretty girls, and with plaques and medals from the elders. When the pageantry was finished, the people were less impressed when I revealed my plan to join with Heshom and his band. They all considered the Machirites reckless and dangerous. However, they praised the man for his boldness at Gath, and no one could deny his bravery or his willingness to undertake hardship. They acknowledged he was a servant of Israel, fair and true, and eagerly anticipated a season of peace.

Publicly, the Benjamites scorned the Judahites for their cowardly betrayal at the Rock of Etam. But privately, I know they sympathized and would have done the same thing. Nevertheless, celebrations were hardly dampened. Even my father's old adversary Zilpah came to congratulate me with the large bald man. That fellow looked at me with sincere admiration, put his arm around me, and said when he considered my treatment of the Philistines, he guessed he got off easy with a deflated testicle.

After a day in Mizpah, I continued north to Shiloh, where I was similarly welcomed by both the Levites and Ephraimites. The Kohathites came and established the tabernacle, and the people sang and worshipped the Lord. I saw the child Samuel serving the high priest Eli, and I thanked the boy for the wisdom he shared on the road to Lehi.

Heshom arrived a day later with little fanfare and less public enthusiasm, but he kept his chin high and his eyes fixed upon the mission. In all discussions, public or private, with one elder or a council of fifty, he affirmed my leadership, praising me as God's chosen vessel to free Israel from oppression. And this is how he truly felt. There was no jealously, no dishonesty in him, no secret agenda. Nor did he covet praise from men; indeed, he concealed that his band, though outnumbered, had cut off the last contingent of retreating Red Bolts until I made the story known.

In short, Heshom had waited nearly his entire life to see a free Israel, and he was determined that nothing should ruin the opportunity at hand.

Dealing respectfully and pragmatically with Shiloh's elders and Eli, he asked for nothing more than a chance to rally an army of the willing behind my banner to fully secure the land. In the weeks that followed, the young men came in droves from all over, including from Judah—these were eager to atone for the weakness of their leaders, and many of them proved exceedingly valiant when their time came.

Heshom knew the Israelites would not accept a tax for our expenses. Consequently, he proposed to lease the Red Bolts' armor and weaponry to the volunteers who lacked their own. His price was more than fair—a pittance, really—and those in need of coins raised support from among their families and villages, such that all of our expenses were easily covered and a steady income obtained. He gave a tenth to the Levites and shared generously with the Kohathites to strengthen the tabernacle. In all of this, Heshom avoided bitter arguments like the one with Macksam. He gained influence and secured future favors. And I should add his daughter, Rya, was an invaluable administrator. I have no patience for such organizing or accounts, and neither did the other men.

Before long, I had silver enough to refund my parents' expenses for my wedding. I also repaid Torgan for his hunting equipment, along with the market equivalent of 300 jackals and other lost income, so that he was exceedingly grateful for my generosity. And yet my funds were hardly depleted.

With my debts paid and my future purpose established, I felt full closure on the former portion of my life. That feeling of adventure that first bedeviled my soul on the journey to Mahaneh Dan crept back into my heart.

Though Heshom and his sons and I eventually had a falling out, I will never forget his clarity of purpose, his self-lessness, or his love of Israel. He was a lone friend when I had no other, and he undertook great personal risk to recover my body from the Philistines when he thought such a chore would be necessary. In a life filled with betrayal, that rare act of fidelity touched my heart and proved his worth.

Moreover, in his company I was possessed of full confidence for the crises to come.

Acknowledgments

I would like to thank Dad, Steve, Nick, and Christen for reviewing early drafts and sharing invaluable criticism. Thank you also to Chris for the steady encouragement throughout the process, and to Tom for the belief. God bless you all.

About the Author

J eff Meredith lives outside Atlanta with his wife, children, and dogs. He enjoys gardening and growing the sorts of fruits and flowers that are prevalent in the Bible (and in this story), especially pomegranates and figs of every color.

Preview Chapter

from Samson, Invincible Foe
Book II in the Testimony of Samson Series

That next morning, early though it was, all Shiloh came out to see off our small army. The older men formed an honor guard and their wives waved pennons as children set flowers and ribbons by the roadside. Levites blew their horns and beat their tambourines. Even old Eli the high priest pulled himself out of bed to croak out a blessing:

Hear, O Israel: Today you are on the verge of battle with your enemies. Do not let your heart faint, do not be afraid, and do not tremble or be terrified because of them; for the Lord your God is he who goes with you, to fight for you against your enemies, to save you.

Thus we left in fanfare and glory, shields and armor shining, spirits soaring, and many of the women watching had tears in their eyes.

On their horses, Heshom and his sons held their spears high, their orange banners snapping sharply in the morning breeze. The rest of us followed quietly and confidently in tow. I rode my prize donkey Carmel, the undeniable herdsire among thirty or so jacks. Several Reubenites had camels, but the multitude went on foot. All together, we were nearly 500 strong.

We made for Aram by way of Shechem and Tirzah, passing to the west of Mt. Gilboa before we reached the oaks at Moreh after four long days, where we rested and revictualed.

Once the dust was out of our nostrils, we cut east through the valley of Jezreel, continuing north alongside the Jordan until we crossed above the Yarmuk. From there we made for Golan, where rascals are never in short supply, but Heshom was well regarded. Then we traveled straight north to Mt. Hermon and set up camp at its southern foot by the ruined city. The dreaded Arameans were nowhere to be found, but certain vagabond shepherds spoke of rumors about raiders in one part or another. And so, the next morning, we followed their vague report northeast, heading along a spotty, rugged trail through the foothills in search of an enemy to fight.

Circling up around the mountain's dry wilderness, we saw no sign of invaders—just the occasional remains of shepherds' camps and abandoned mines. After five uneventful days winding up and down a number of sparse and desolate valleys, we arrived northeast of Mt. Hermon. Heshom informed us that Damascus itself was not far off. He pointed to a rounded ridge due east, where he said one could look down upon the old city, as indeed he had. Some of the boys said we ought to go roll stones on those idol worshippers. Others, being emboldened by their armor, argued we should surprise the enemy, seize the city, and put a lasting end to their transgressions—*then* we would have a name for ourselves!

Heshom refused to dignify such nonsense with any response, insisting only that we would continue on our path around the mountain, and if there were no enemies to fight, so much the better, because it meant our brothers were living in peace.

His passive answer disappointed everyone. We had been on the move for more than a fortnight, but the promise of high adventure appeared an empty one. Each day was like the last: a hot, plodding trek through uneven, rocky terrain, without even a hint of any enemy.

Heshom poured more salt in the wound a morning or two later when he announced that, as we were now at our farthest point north and low on flour, we must go on half rations until we could resupply in Ijon, a small, ramshackle town all the way back on the southern side of Mt. Hermon. Most of us had already been scrimping by on crumbs, and the groaning from the rank and file intensified, especially from those on foot who had not packed as abundantly. Heshom was in no mood for arguing; from high atop his horse he chastised us all, saying, "You wanted to be men at arms. Your heart was set on the good and glory of Israel. What happened? A little hardship—you must dine lightly, God forbid!—and now you ask to trade away your swords and armor for forks and vittles? If you wanted to indulge your bellies, you should have mustered into a fat merchant's kitchen."

All of this may have been true, but it was hardly motivating to so many raw, hungry recruits, and they began to grumble and sulk among themselves.

Annoyance with both the "steward" and the "laborers," coupled with my own empty stomach, led me to take an attitude as well, and I expressed a keen wish to be free from everyone. While the others ate their meager meals, I made my way on foot for an outcropping of rock roughly one arrow's flight down the slope, answering Heshom's sons abruptly that I was leaving for a moment's privacy, *if* that was all right with them. And indeed, that is all I intended—but the firstborn, Ranun, followed me in awkward silence.

As we came near the line of broken boulders, he said to me doubtfully, "Samson, do you believe my father handles the men correctly?"

I snapped, "How should I know? I have no experience in such things. They are acting like spoiled children, and your father is lording it over them like the Machirite he is."

"Yes, that is my concern, and——" he suddenly raised his head and sniffed intently. "Samson, what *is* that?"

As far as I could tell: Savory smoke and grilled meat, fired to perfection. Having eaten nothing but dusty bread for two weeks, the smell promised a feast worthy of Esau's birthright, if ever there was one. We took in the aroma deeply and greedily, following it like a couple of eager hounds, bounding down haphazard pilings of granite rubble, until we came around a large boulder—and stumbled right into five hard-bitten brigands! They lay in their armor, feasting on lamb and dipping cardoons in butter. We stopped in our tracks and cried out in surprise, "Who are you?"

They were just as startled to see us. Once the shock wore off their faces, they looked suspiciously among themselves until the closest finally spoke up. "As you can plainly see," he said coldly, gesturing to a mere three or four nearby sheep, "we are shepherds from around these parts. Who are you?" And he bit off a hunk of meat, feigning indifference to our interruption as he slid a hand stealthily toward his sword.

"You smell like shepherds, but what a pity your flock is so piddly," I said, walking toward them slowly. "Strange that you look like Arameans. If you really are herdsmen, where are your crooks?"

With that, we pounced! Ranun unsheathed his sword and leapt at the man who spoke with us, and they rolled in the rocky grass in mortal struggle. I lunged at the remnant as they stood to fight. Having brought no weapon, I grabbed two of the men and slammed their heads together so that they fell face first into the dirt and died. Picking up one of their clubs, I struck another over the head, and he also bit the dust. This happened as Ranun ran his foe through, leaving just one of the Arameans. He turned to run, but we caught him and secured him with his own rope. After feasting on the remainder of their breakfast, we forced our prisoner to walk before us, returning to our army with the tiny flock in tow.

Back at camp, we were given a hero's welcome, not for our victory or our prisoner, but for the presumably delicious plunder. However, Heshom would not allow a single sheep to be slaughtered, much to everyone's grief—besides me and Ranun, who were already well satisfied on our prisoner's choice roast. Heshom questioned the man and learned the main contingent of Arameans was less than a mile ahead. Then he slit his throat and threw him down the steepest part of the hill, ordering all the men to arm themselves, for the real fight was near. The Israelites were fierce with hunger; if there was still to be no decent meal until a battle was won, then at least all would have motivation to gird themselves like men.

By lot we chose four unwilling ones to keep the animals— only Heshom and his sons remained mounted. Rapidly now we advanced over the same trail Ranun and I had traveled an hour earlier, continuing in silence past the enemy's smoldering campfire and their strewn bodies, steadily descending through a narrow, veined valley that rose slightly again at the bottom as it curved west round the mountain's skirt. Sensing battle, we broadened our formation to a loose fifty-man front and climbed up together.

A gently sloping vista opened before us, and there at last! Scattered over the meadow like a vast herd at rest were the Arameans.

Some two thousand strong, they were enjoying a leisurely morning, eating or lying about in small groups, or else tending the sheep, goats, and oxen they had raided. And they were utterly bewildered by our appearance. Apparently, the small group Ranun and I had taken was the scouting guard, for no one in this camp was prepared for battle, least of all from the direction of their own country.

As they ran for their swords, Heshom cried out, "For the Lord and for Israel!" We answered in kind, and charged headlong into their ranks, routing them and inflicting great slaughter. I was positioned in the middle of our line, with a sword in one hand and a club in the other, and I outran them all in my zeal to punish these pillagers, crashing into a group of wavering Arameans where I stabbed bellies and busted heads. The rest followed behind and did likewise, and our enemies panicked and fled. On their horses, Heshom and his sons raced down our flank, trampling and spearing the raiders or else herding stragglers toward our ready swords.

We chased them down the slope for nearly two miles, cutting down hundreds upon hundreds of men as mercilessly as they had treated our brother Naphtalites and Manassites, leaving their dead scattered over the face of the mountain. The ground became increasingly broken with canyons and rocky outcroppings, slowing our pursuit—until we reached the cliffs that overlook the headwaters of the Jordan where it is little more than a shallow creek. The Arameans' escape was cut off there, and we threw down the last of them on the rocks below where they were dashed to pieces. A mere handful escaped by climbing out of range of our arrows. Some of our more spirited runners begged to pursue, but Heshom said to leave them; it would better serve us if a few lived to tell their countrymen of this disaster. Perhaps that might keep them away for a longer time.

Afterward we gathered up the flocks and herds, which scattered rather widely during the battle, and returned to the Arameans' campsite delirious with the joy of our first victory. Heshom beamed like a proud father. The arguments from that morning about rationing were far from our minds as we made sacrifices to the Lord and enjoyed a rich feast as champions of Israel.

Our casualties were exceedingly light: only nine killed, one of whom fell on his own sword in the excitement of the chase.

We took from the enemy more than 500 swords, 50 spears, 200 bronze shields, countless spiked clubs, myriad gold and silver trinkets, blankets, sandals, tunics, and other valuables. Out of these considerable rewards, Heshom reserved the first tenth for God and two-tenths for the subsistence of our company. The remainder was divided among the men straight away. Since the Arameans outnumbered us by more than four to one, all were well pleased with their share of the spoils.

Heshom dispatched his youngest son, Gabriel, and several others to ride ahead and proclaim the good news to the people of Kedesh and Beth Anath, and to begin establishing the rightful owners of the recovered livestock.

Through this adventure, I carried no more than one man's load. Yes, I led the charge and stayed at the forefront of the fighting. When my brothers saw me strike down the first group of Arameans, they took heart for the battle and followed, charging with reckless bravery and earning the cuts and bruises that proved their valor. The Lord was with us one and all, and this was a victory for the entirety of Israel. After forty years of suffering, he saw fit to give his people rest. He put our enemies into our hands, and we slaughtered them from vanguard to rearguard and spearhead to bounty.

In all of this, Heshom did nothing without confiding in me. He initiated no specific plan or even gave a general order unless we had discussed the matter first, because he recognized that I was God's chosen instrument for these purposes. This was right and good for him to do, but it was mere formality. Planning and organization did not hold my interest. I longed only for the fight, and the Lord had just begun to fulfill that craving...

CPSIA information can be obtained
at www.ICGtesting.com
Printed in the USA
LVHW050444041121
702355LV00014BA/63

9 781950 948826